EAS

D1579082

Get **more** out of libraries

Please return or renew this item by the last date shown.

You can renew online at www.hants.gov.uk/library

Or by phoning 0300 555 1387

C016008011

The Dream Woman

Wilkie Collins

ALMA CLASSICS

ALMA CLASSICS LTD
London House
243-253 Lower Mortlake Road
Richmond
Surrey TW9 2LL
United Kingdom
www.almaclassics.com

The Dream Woman first published as *The Ostler* in *Household Words* in 1855
This edition first published by Alma Books Ltd in 2015

Extra Material © Alma Classics Ltd

Cover image © Sara Proietti

Printed and bound by CPI Group (UK) Ltd, Croydon, CR0 4YY

ISBN: 978-1-84749-406-1

Contents

Wilkie Collins (1824–89)

William Collins,
Wilkie's father

Harriet Collins,
Wilkie's mother

Caroline Graves

Martha Rudd

Wilkie Collins as a child, sketched by William Collins (top left),
and in an 1851 oil painting by J.E. Millais

Detail from a draft manuscript of
Wilkie Collins's 1852 novel *Basil*

Wilkie Collins's house in
Gloucester Place, London

The Dream Woman

A Mystery, in Four Narratives

Introductory Note

The original version of this story was published, many years since, in *Household Words*, and was afterwards printed in the collection of my shorter stories called *The Queen of Hearts*. In the present version – written for my public readings in the United States – new characters and new incidents are introduced; and a new beginning and ending have been written. Indeed, the whole complexion of the narrative differs so essentially from the older and shorter version, as to justify me in believing that the reader will find in these pages what is, to all practical intents and purposes, a new story.

– W.C.

Persons of the Mystery

FRANCIS RAVEN — *Ostler*

MRS RAVEN — *His mother*

MRS CHANCE — *His aunt*

PERCY FAIRBANK

MRS FAIRBANK — *His master and mistress*

JOSEPH RIGOBERT — *His fellow servant*

ALICIA WARLOCK — *His wife*

PERIOD — THE PRESENT TIME

SCENE — PARTLY IN ENGLAND,
PARTLY IN FRANCE

The First Narrative

INTRODUCTORY STATEMENT OF THE FACTS.
BY PERCY FAIRBANK.

1

"HULLO, THERE! Ostler! Hullo-o-o!"

"My dear! Why don't you look for the bell?"

"I *have* looked – there is no bell."

"And nobody in the yard. How very extraordinary! Call again, dear."

"Ostler! Hullo, there! Ostler-r-r!"

My second call echoes through empty space, and rouses nobody – produces, in short, no visible result. I am at the end of my resources – I don't know what to say or what to do next. Here I stand in the solitary inn yard of a strange town, with two horses to hold, and a lady to take care of. By way of adding to my responsibilities, it so happens that one of the horses is dead lame, and that the lady is my wife.

Who am I? – you will ask.

There is plenty of time to answer the question. Nothing happens; and nobody appears to receive us. Let me introduce myself and my wife.

I am Percy Fairbank – English gentleman – age (let us say) forty – no profession – moderate politics – middle height – fair complexion – easy character – plenty of money.

My wife is a French lady. She was Mademoiselle Clotilde Delorge – when I was first presented to her at her father's house in France. I fell in love with her – I really don't know why. It might have been because I was perfectly idle, and had nothing else to do at the time. Or it might have been because all my friends said she was the very last woman whom I ought to think of marrying. On the surface, I must own, there is nothing in common between Mrs Fairbank and me. She is tall; she is dark; she is nervous, excitable, romantic; in all her opinions she proceeds to extremes. What could such a woman see in me? What could I see in her? I know no more than you do. In some mysterious manner we exactly suit each other. We have been man and wife for ten years, and our only regret is that we have no children. I don't know what *you* may think; *I* call that – upon the whole – a happy marriage.

So much for ourselves. The next question is – what has brought us into the inn yard? And why am I obliged to turn groom, and hold the horses?

We live for the most part in France – at the country house in which my wife and I first met. Occasionally, by way of variety, we pay visits to my friends in England. We are paying one of those visits now. Our host is an old college friend of mine, possessed of a fine estate in Somersetshire; and we have arrived at his house – called Farleigh Hall – towards the close of the hunting season.

On the day of which I am now writing – destined to be a memorable day in our calendar – the hounds meet at Farleigh Hall. Mrs Fairbank and I are mounted on two of the best horses in my friend's stables. We are quite unworthy of that distinction; for we know nothing, and care nothing, about hunting. On the other hand, we delight in riding, and we enjoy the breezy spring morning and the fair and fertile English landscape surrounding us on every side. While the hunt prospers, we follow the hunt. But when a check occurs – when time passes and patience is sorely tried; when the bewildered dogs run hither and thither and strong language falls from the lips of exasperated sportsmen – we fail to take any further interest in the proceedings. We turn our horses' heads in the direction of a grassy lane, delightfully shaded by trees. We trot merrily along the lane, and find ourselves on an open common. We gallop across the common, and follow the windings of a second lane. We cross a brook, we pass through a village, we emerge into pastoral solitude among the hills. The horses toss their heads, and neigh to each other, and enjoy it as much as we do. The hunt is forgotten. We are as happy as a couple of children; we are actually singing a French song – when in one moment our merriment comes to an end. My wife's horse sets one of his forefeet on a loose stone, and stumbles. His rider's ready hand saves him from falling. But, at the first attempt he makes to go on, the sad truth shows itself – a tendon is strained; the horse is lame.

What is to be done? We are strangers in a lonely part of the country. Look where we may, we see no signs of a human habitation. There is nothing for it but to take the bridle road up the hill, and try what we can discover on the other side. I transfer the saddles, and mount my wife on my own horse. He is not used to carry a lady; he misses the familiar pressure of a man's legs on either side of him; he fidgets, and starts, and kicks up the dust.

I follow on foot, at a respectful distance from his heels, leading the lame horse. Is there a more miserable object on the face of creation than a lame horse? I have seen lame men and lame dogs who were cheerful creatures; but I never yet saw a lame horse who didn't look heartbroken over his own misfortune.

For half an hour my wife capers and curvets sideways along the bridle road. I trudge on behind her, and the heartbroken horse halts behind *me*. Hard by the top of the hill, our melancholy procession passes a Somersetshire peasant at work in a field. I summon the man to approach us; and the man looks at me stolidly, from the middle of the field, without stirring a step. I ask at the top of my voice how far it is to Farleigh Hall. The Somersetshire peasant answers at the top of *his* voice:

"Vourteen mile. Gi' oi a drap o' zyder."

I translate (for my wife's benefit) from the Somersetshire language into the English language. We are fourteen miles from Farleigh Hall, and our friend in the field desires to be rewarded for giving us that information, with a drop of cider. There is the peasant, painted by himself! Quite a bit of character, my dear! Quite a bit of character!

Mrs Fairbank doesn't view the study of agricultural human nature with my relish. Her fidgety horse will not allow her a moment's repose; she is beginning to lose her temper.

"We can't go fourteen miles in this way," she says. "Where is the nearest inn? Ask that brute in the field!"

I take a shilling from my pocket and hold it up in the sun. The shilling exercises magnetic virtues. The shilling draws the peasant slowly towards me from the middle of the field. I inform him that we want to put up the horses, and to hire a carriage to take us back to Farleigh Hall. Where can we do that? The peasant answers (with his eye on the shilling):

"At Oonderbridge, to be zure." (At Underbridge, to be sure.)

"Is it far to Underbridge?"

The peasant repeats, "Var to Oonderbridge?" – and laughs at the question. "Hoo-hoo-hoo!" (Underbridge is evidently close by – if we could only find it.)

"Will you show us the way, my man?"

"Will you gi' oi a drap o' zyder?"

I courteously bend my head, and point to the shilling. The agricultural intelligence exerts itself. The peasant joins our melancholy procession. My wife is a fine woman, but he never once looks at my wife – and, more extraordinary still, he never even looks at the horses. His eyes are with his mind – and his mind is on the shilling.

We reach the top of the hill – and behold, on the other side, nestling in a valley, the shrine of our pilgrimage, the town of Underbridge! Here our guide claims his shilling, and leaves us to find out the inn for ourselves. I am constitutionally a polite man. I say "Good morning" at parting. The guide looks at me with the shilling between his teeth to make sure that it is a good one. "Marnin'!" he says savagely – and turns his back on us, as if we had offended him. A curious product, this, of the growth of civilization. If I didn't see a church spire at Underbridge, I might suppose that we had lost ourselves on a savage island.

2

ARRIVING AT THE TOWN, we have no difficulty in finding the inn. The town is composed of one desolate street, and midway in that street stands the inn – an ancient stone building sadly out of repair. The painting on the signboard is obliterated. The shutters over the long range of front windows are all closed. A cock and his hens are the only living creatures at the door. Plainly, this is one of the old inns of the stagecoach period, ruined by the railway. We pass through the open arched doorway, and find no one to welcome us. We advance into the stable yard behind; I assist my wife to dismount – and there we are in the position already disclosed to view at the opening of this narrative. No bell to ring. No human creature to answer when I call. I stand helpless, with the bridles of the horses in my hand. Mrs Fairbank saunters gracefully down the length of the yard, and does – what all women do when they find themselves in a strange place. She opens every door as she passes it, and peeps in. On my side, I have just recovered my breath, I am on the point of shouting for the ostler for the third and last time, when I hear Mrs Fairbank suddenly call to me.

"Percy! Come here!"

Her voice is eager and agitated. She has opened a last door at the end of the yard, and has started back from some sight which has suddenly met her view. I hitch the horses' bridles on a rusty nail in the wall near me, and join my wife. She has turned pale, and catches me nervously by the arm.

"Good Heavens!" she cries. "Look at that!"

I look – and what do I see?

I see a dingy little stable, containing two stalls. In one stall a horse is munching his corn. In the other a man is lying asleep on the litter.

A worn, withered, woebegone man in an ostler's dress. His hollow wrinkled cheeks, his scanty grizzled hair, his dry yellow skin, tell their own tale of past sorrow or suffering. There is an ominous frown on his eyebrows – there is a painful nervous contraction on one side of his mouth. I hear him breathing convulsively when I first look in; he shudders and sighs in his sleep. It is not a pleasant sight to see, and I turn round instinctively to the bright sunlight in the yard. My wife turns me back again in the direction of the stable door.

"Wait!" she says. "Wait! He may do it again."

"Do what again?"

"He was talking in his sleep, Percy, when I first looked in. He was dreaming some dreadful dream. Hush! He's beginning again."

I look and listen. The man stirs on his miserable bed. The man speaks, in a quick fierce whisper, through his clenched teeth. "Wake up! Wake up, there! Murder!"

There is an interval of silence. He moves one lean arm slowly until it rests over his throat; he shudders, and turns on his straw; he raises his arm from his throat, and feebly stretches it out; his hand clutches at the straw on the side towards which he has turned; he seems to fancy that he is grasping at the edge of something; I see his lips begin to move again; I step softly into the stable; my wife follows me, with her hand fast clasped in mine. We both bend over him. He is talking once more in his sleep – strange talk, mad talk, this time.

"Light-grey eyes" (we hear him say) "and a droop in the left eyelid – flaxen hair, with a gold-yellow streak in it – all right, mother! Fair, white arms with a down on them – little, lady's hand, with a reddish look round the fingernails – the knife – the cursed knife – first on one side, then on the other – aha, you she-devil! Where is the knife?"

He stops and grows restless on a sudden. We see him writhing on the straw. He throws up both his hands and gasps hysterically for breath. His eyes open suddenly. For a moment they look at nothing, with a vacant glitter in them – then they close again in deeper sleep. Is he dreaming still? Yes, but the dream seems to have taken a new course. When he speaks next, the tone is altered; the words are few – sadly and imploringly repeated over and over again. "Say you love me! I am so fond of *you*. Say you love me! Say you love me!" He sinks into deeper and deeper sleep, faintly repeating those words. They die away on his lips. He speaks no more.

By this time, Mrs Fairbank has got over her terror. She is devoured by curiosity now. The miserable creature on the straw has appealed to the imaginative side of her character. Her illimitable appetite for romance hungers and thirsts for more. She shakes me impatiently by the arm. "Do you hear? There is a woman at the bottom of it, Percy! There is love and murder in it, Percy! Where are the people of the inn? Go into the yard, and call to them again."

My wife belongs, on her mother's side, to the south of France. The south of France breeds fine women with hot tempers. I say no more. Married men will understand my position. Single men may need to be told that there are occasions when we must not only love and honour – we must also obey – our wives.

I turn to the door to obey *my* wife, and find myself confronting a stranger who has stolen on us unawares.

The stranger is a tiny, sleepy, rosy old man, with a vacant pudding face and a shining bald head. He wears drab breeches and gaiters, and a respectable square-tailed ancient black coat. I feel instinctively that here is the landlord of the inn.

"Good morning, sir," says the rosy old man. "I'm a little hard of hearing. Was it you that was a-calling just now in the yard?"

Before I can answer, my wife interposes. She insists (in a shrill voice, adapted to our host's hardness of hearing) on knowing who that unfortunate person is sleeping on the straw? "Where does he come from? Why does he say such dreadful things in his sleep? Is he married or single? Did he ever fall in love with a murderess? What sort of a looking woman was she? Did she really stab him or not? In short, dear Mr Landlord, tell us the whole story!"

Dear Mr Landlord waits drowsily until Mrs Fairbank has quite done – then delivers himself of his reply as follows:

"His name's Francis Raven. He's an Independent Methodist. He was forty-five year old last birthday. And he's my ostler. That's his story."

My wife's hot southern temper finds its way to her foot, and expresses itself by a stamp on the stable yard.

The landlord turns himself sleepily round, and looks at the horses. "A fine pair of horses, them two in the yard. Do you want to put 'em up in my stables?" I reply in the affirmative by a nod. The landlord, bent on making himself agreeable to my wife, addresses her once more. "I'm a-going to wake Francis Raven. He's an Independent Methodist. He was forty-five year old last birthday. And he's my ostler. That's his story."

Having issued this second edition of his interesting narrative, the landlord enters the stable. We follow him, to see how he will wake Francis Raven, and what will happen upon that. The stable broom stands in a corner; the landlord takes it – advances towards the sleeping ostler – and coolly stirs the man up with the broom as if he was a wild beast in a cage. Francis Raven starts to his feet with a cry of terror – looks at us wildly, with a horrid glare of suspicion in his eyes – recovers himself the next moment – and suddenly changes into a decent, quiet, respectable servingman.

"I beg your pardon, ma'am. I beg your pardon, sir."

The tone and manner in which he makes his apologies are both above his apparent station in life. I begin to catch the infection of Mrs Fairbank's interest in this man. We both follow him out into the yard to see what he will do with the horses. The manner in which he lifts the injured leg of the lame horse tells me at once that he understands his business. Quickly and quietly, he leads the animals into an empty stable; quickly and quietly, he gets a bucket of hot water and puts the lame horse's leg into it. "The warm water will reduce the swelling, sir. I will bandage the leg afterward." All that he does, is done intelligently; all that he says, he says to the purpose. Nothing wild, nothing strange about him now. Is this the same man whom we heard talking in his sleep? The same man who woke with that cry of terror and that horrid suspicion in his eyes? I determine to try him with one or two questions.

3

"NOT MUCH TO DO HERE," I say to the ostler. "Very little to do sir," the ostler replies.

"Anybody staying in the house?"

"The house is quite empty, sir."

"I thought you were all dead. I could make nobody hear me."

"The landlord is very deaf, sir, and the waiter is out on an errand."

"Yes – and *you* were fast asleep in the stable. Do you often take a nap in the daytime?"

The worn face of the ostler faintly flushes. His eyes look away from my eyes for the first time. Mrs Fairbank furtively pinches my arm. Are we on the eve of a discovery at last? I repeat my question. The man has no civil alternative but to give me an answer. The answer is given in these words:

"I was tired out, sir. You wouldn't have found me asleep in the daytime but for that."

"Tired out, eh? You had been hard at work, I suppose?"

"No, sir."

"What was it, then?"

He hesitates again, and answers unwillingly, "I was up all night."

"Up all night? Anything going on in the town?"

"Nothing going on, sir."

"Anybody ill?"

"Nobody ill, sir."

That reply is the last. Try as I may, I can extract nothing more from him. He turns away and busies himself in attending to the horse's leg. I leave the stable, to speak to the landlord about the carriage which is to take us back to Farleigh Hall. Mrs Fairbank remains with the ostler, and favours me with a look at parting. The look says plainly, "*I* mean to find out why he was up all night. Leave him to *me*."

The ordering of the carriage is easily accomplished. The inn possesses one horse and one chaise. The landlord has a story to tell of the horse, and a story to tell of the chaise. They resemble the story of Francis Raven – with this exception, that the horse and chaise belong to no religious persuasion. "The horse will be nine year old next birthday. I've had the shay for four and twenty year. Mr Max of Underbridge, he bred the horse; and Mr Pooley of Yeovil, he built the shay. It's my horse and my shay. And that's *their* story!" Having relieved his mind of these details, the landlord proceeds to put the harness on the horse. By way of assisting him, I drag the chaise into the yard. Just as our preparations are completed, Mrs Fairbank appears. A moment or two later the ostler follows her out. He has bandaged the horse's leg, and is now ready to drive us to Farleigh Hall. I observe signs of agitation in his face and manner, which suggest that my wife has found her way into his confidence. I put the question to her privately in a corner of the yard. "Well? Have you found out why Francis Raven was up all night?"

Mrs Fairbank has an eye to dramatic effect. Instead of answering plainly, Yes or No, she suspends the interest and excites the audience by putting a question on her side.

"What is the day of the month, dear?"

"The day of the month is the first of March."

"The first of March, Percy, is Francis Raven's birthday."

I try to look as if I was interested – and don't succeed.

"Francis was born," Mrs Fairbank proceeds gravely, "at two o'clock in the morning."

I begin to wonder whether my wife's intellect is going the way of the landlord's intellect. "Is that all?" I ask.

"It is *not* all," Mrs Fairbank answers. "Francis Raven sits up on the morning of his birthday, because he is afraid to go to bed."

"And why is he afraid to go to bed?"

"Because he is in peril of his life."

"On his birthday?"

"On his birthday. At two o'clock in the morning. As regularly as the birthday comes round."

There she stops. Has she discovered no more than that? No more thus far. I begin to feel really interested by this time. I ask eagerly what it means? Mrs Fairbank points mysteriously to the chaise – with Francis Raven (hitherto our ostler, now our coachman) waiting for us to get in. The chaise has a seat for two in front, and a seat for one behind. My wife casts a warning look at me, and places herself on the seat in front.

The necessary consequence of this arrangement is that Mrs Fairbank sits by the side of the driver, during a journey of two hours and more. Need I state the result? It would be an insult to your intelligence to state the result. Let me offer you my place in the chaise. And let Francis Raven tell his terrible story in his own words.

The Second Narrative

4

I T IS NOW TEN YEARS AGO since I got my first warning of the great trouble of my life, in the Vision of a Dream.

I shall be better able to tell you about it, if you will please suppose yourselves to be drinking tea along with us in our little cottage in Cambridgeshire, ten years since.

The time was the close of day, and there were three of us at the table, namely, my mother, myself and my mother's sister, Mrs Chance. These two were Scotchwomen by birth, and both were widows. There was no other resemblance between them that I can call to mind. My mother had lived all her life in England, and had no more of the Scotch brogue on her tongue than I have. My aunt Chance had never been out of Scotland until she came to keep house with my mother after her husband's death. And

23

when *she* opened her lips you heard broad Scotch, I can tell you, if ever you heard it yet!

As it fell out, there was a matter of some consequence in debate among us that evening. It was this: whether I should do well or not to take a long journey on foot the next morning.

Now the next morning happened to be the day before my birthday; and the purpose of the journey was to offer myself for a situation as groom at a great house in the neighbouring county to ours. The place was reported as likely to fall vacant in about three weeks' time. I was as well fitted to fill it as any other man. In the prosperous days of our family, my father had been manager of a training stable, and he had kept me employed among the horses from my boyhood upwards. Please to excuse my troubling you with these small matters. They all fit into my story further on, as you will soon find out.

My poor mother was dead against my leaving home on the morrow.

"You can never walk all the way there and all the way back again by tomorrow night," she says. "The end of it will be that you will sleep away from home on your birthday. You have never done that yet, Francis, since your father's death. I don't like your doing it now. Wait a day longer, my son – only one day."

For my own part, I was weary of being idle, and I couldn't abide the notion of delay. Even one day might make all the difference. Some other man might take time by the forelock and get the place.

"Consider how long I have been out of work," I says, "and don't ask me to put off the journey. I won't fail you, mother. I'll get back by tomorrow night, if I have to pay my last sixpence for a lift in a cart."

My mother shook her head. "I don't like it, Francis – I don't like it!" There was no moving her from that view. We argued and argued, until we were both at a deadlock. It ended in our agreeing to refer the difference between us to my mother's sister, Mrs Chance.

While we were trying hard to convince each other, my aunt Chance sat as dumb as a fish, stirring her tea and thinking her own thoughts. When we made our appeal to her, she seemed, as it were, to wake up. "Ye baith refer it to my puir judgement?" she says, in her broad Scotch. We both answered Yes. Upon that my aunt Chance first cleared the tea table, and then pulled out from the pocket of her gown a pack of cards.

Don't run away, if you please, with the notion that this was done lightly, with a view to amuse my mother and me. My aunt Chance seriously believed that she could look into the future by telling fortunes on the cards. She did nothing herself without first consulting the cards. She could give no more serious proof of her interest in my welfare than the proof which she was offering now. I don't say it profanely; I only mention the fact – the cards had, in some incomprehensible way, got themselves jumbled up together with her religious convictions. You meet with people nowadays who believe in spirits working by way of tables and chairs. On the same principle (if there *is* any principle in it) my aunt Chance believed in Providence working by way of the cards.

"Whether *you* are right, Francie, or your mither – whether ye will do weel or ill, the morrow, to go or stay – the cairds will tell it. We are a' in the hands of Proavidence. The cairds will tell it."

Hearing this, my mother turned her head aside, with something of a sour look in her face. Her sister's notions about the cards were little better than flat blasphemy to her mind. But she kept her opinion to herself. My aunt Chance, to own the truth, had inherited, through her late husband, a pension of thirty pounds a year. This was an important contribution to our housekeeping, and we poor relations were bound to treat her with a certain respect. As for myself, if my poor father never did anything else for me before he fell into difficulties, he gave me a good education, and raised me (thank God) above superstitions of all sorts. However, a very little amused me in those days, and I waited to have my fortune told as patiently as if I believed in it too!

My aunt began her hocus-pocus by throwing out all the cards in the pack under seven. She shuffled the rest, with her left hand, for luck, and then she gave them to me to cut. "Wi' yer left hand, Francie. Mind that! Pet yer trust in Proavidence – but dinna forget that yer luck's in yer left hand!" A long and roundabout shifting of the cards followed, reducing them in number, until there were just fifteen of them left, laid out neatly before my aunt in a half-circle. The card which happened to lay outermost, at the right-hand end of the circle, was, according to rule in such cases, the card chosen to represent me. By way of being appropriate to my situation as a poor groom out of work, the card was – the King of Diamonds.

"I tak' up the King o' Diamants," says my aunt. "I count seven cairds fra' richt to left; and I humbly ask a blessing on what follows." My aunt shut her eyes as if she was saying grace before meat, and held up to me the seventh card. I called the seventh card – the Queen of Spades. My aunt opened her eyes again in a hurry, and cast a sly look my way. "The Queen o' Spades means a dairk woman. Ye'll be thinking in secret, Francie, of a dairk woman?"

When a man has been out of place for more than three months, his mind isn't troubled much with thinking of women – light or dark. I was thinking of the groom's place at the great house, and I tried to say so. My aunt Chance wouldn't listen. She treated my interruption with contempt. "Hoot-toot! There's the caird in your hand! If ye're no thinking of her the day, ye'll be thinking of her the morrow. Where's the harm of thinking of a dairk woman! I was aince a dairk woman myself, before my hair was grey. Haud yer peace, Francie, and watch the cairds."

I watched the cards as I was told. There were seven left on the table. My aunt removed two from one end of the row and two from the other, and desired me to call the two outermost of the three cards now left on the table. I called the Ace of Clubs and the Ten of Diamonds. My aunt

Chance lifted her eyes to the ceiling with a look of devout gratitude which sorely tried my mother's patience. The Ace of Clubs and the Ten of Diamonds, taken together, signified: first, good news (evidently the news of the groom's place!); secondly, a journey that lay before me (pointing plainly to my journey tomorrow!); thirdly and lastly, a sum of money (probably the groom's wages!) waiting to find its way into my pockets. Having told my fortune in these encouraging terms, my aunt declined to carry the experiment any further. "Eh, lad! it's a clean tempting of Proavidence to ask mair o' the cairds than the cairds have tauld us noo. Gae yer ways tomorrow to the great hoose. A dairk woman will meet ye at the gate, and she'll have a hand in getting ye the groom's place, wi' a' the gratifications and pairquisites appertaining to the same. And, mebbe, when yer poaket's full o' mony, ye'll no' be forgetting yer aunt Chance, maintaining her ain unbleemished widowhood – wi' Proavidence assisting – on thratty punds a year!"

I promised to remember my aunt Chance (who had the defect, by the way, of being a terribly greedy person after money) on the next happy occasion when my poor empty pockets were to be filled at last. This done, I looked at my mother. She had agreed to take her sister for umpire between us, and her sister had given it in my favour. She raised no more objections. Silently, she got on her feet, and kissed me, and sighed bitterly – and so left the room. My aunt Chance shook her head. "I doubt, Francie, yer puir mither has but a heathen notion of the vairtue of the cairds!"

By daylight the next morning I set forth on my journey. I looked back at the cottage as I opened the garden gate. At one window was my mother, with her handkerchief to her eyes. At the other stood my aunt Chance, holding up the Queen of Spades by way of encouraging me at starting. I waved my hand to both of them in token of farewell, and stepped out briskly into the road. It was then the last day of February. Be pleased to remember, in connection with this, that the first of March was the day, and two o'clock in the morning the hour, of my birth.

5

Now you know how I came to leave home. The next thing to tell is, what happened on the journey. I reached the great house in reasonably good time considering the distance. At the very first trial of it, the prophecy of the cards turned out to be wrong. The person

who met me at the lodge gate was not a dark woman –
in fact, not a woman at all – but a boy. He directed me
on the way to the servants' offices – and there again the
cards were all wrong. I encountered, not one woman, but
three – and not one of the three was dark. I have stated
that I am not superstitious, and I have told the truth. But
I must own that I did feel a certain fluttering at the heart
when I made my bow to the steward, and told him what
business had brought me to the house. His answer completed the discomfiture of Aunt Chance's fortune-telling.
My ill luck still pursued me. That very morning another
man had applied for the groom's place, and had got it.

I swallowed my disappointment as well as I could, and
thanked the steward, and went to the inn in the village to
get the rest and food which I sorely needed by this time.

Before starting on my homeward walk I made some
enquiries at the inn, and ascertained that I might save
a few miles, on my return, by following a new road.
Furnished with full instructions, several times repeated,
as to the various turnings I was to take, I set forth, and
walked on till the evening with only one stoppage for
bread and cheese. Just as it was getting towards dark,
the rain came on and the wind began to rise; and I found

myself, to make matters worse, in a part of the country with which I was entirely unacquainted, though I guessed myself to be some fifteen miles from home. The first house I found to enquire at was a lonely roadside inn, standing on the outskirts of a thick wood. Solitary as the place looked, it was welcome to a lost man who was also hungry, thirsty, footsore and wet. The landlord was civil and respectable-looking, and the price he asked for a bed was reasonable enough. I was grieved to disappoint my mother. But there was no conveyance to be had, and I could go no further afoot that night. My weariness fairly forced me to stop at the inn.

I may say for myself that I am a temperate man. My supper simply consisted of some rashers of bacon, a slice of home-made bread and a pint of ale. I did not go to bed immediately after this moderate meal, but sat up with the landlord, talking about my bad prospects and my long run of ill luck, and diverging from these topics to the subjects of horseflesh and racing. Nothing was said either by myself, my host or the few labourers who strayed into the taproom which could, in the slightest degree, excite my mind or set my fancy – which is only a small fancy at the best of times – playing tricks with my common sense.

At a little after eleven the house was closed. I went round with the landlord, and held the candle while the doors and lower windows were being secured. I noticed with surprise the strength of the bolts, bars and iron-sheathed shutters.

"You see, we are rather lonely here," says the landlord. "We never have had any attempts to break in yet, but it's always as well to be on the safe side. When nobody is sleeping here, I am the only man in the house. My wife and daughter are timid, and the servant girl takes after her missuses. Another glass of ale, before you turn in? – no? Well, how such a sober man as you comes to be out of place is more than I can understand for one. Here's where you're to sleep. You're the only lodger tonight, and I think you'll say my missus has done her best to make you comfortable. You're quite sure you won't have another glass of ale? – very well. Goodnight."

It was half-past eleven by the clock in the passage as we went upstairs to the bedroom. The window looked out on the wood at the back of the house.

I locked my door, set my candle on the chest of drawers and wearily got me ready for bed. The bleak wind was still blowing, and the solemn, surging moan of it in the wood was very dreary to hear through the night silence. Feeling strangely wakeful, I resolved to keep the candle alight until I began to grow sleepy. The truth is, I was not quite myself. I was depressed in mind by my disappointment of the morning; and I was worn out in body by my long walk. Between the two, I own I couldn't face the prospect of lying awake in the darkness, listening to the dismal moan of the wind in the wood.

Sleep stole on me before I was aware of it; my eyes closed, and I fell off to rest, without having so much as thought of extinguishing the candle.

The next thing that I remember was a faint shivering that ran through me from head to foot, and a dreadful sinking pain at my heart, such as I had never felt before. The shivering only disturbed my slumbers – the pain woke me instantly. In one moment I passed from a state of sleep to a state of wakefulness – my eyes wide open – my mind clear on a sudden as if by a miracle.

The candle had burnt down nearly to the last morsel of tallow, but the unsnuffed wick had just fallen off, and the light was, for the moment, fair and full.

Between the foot of the bed and the closed door, I saw a person in my room. The person was a woman, standing looking at me, with a knife in her hand.

It does no credit to my courage to confess it – but the truth *is* the truth. I was struck speechless with terror. There I lay with my eyes on the woman; there the woman stood (with the knife in her hand) with *her* eyes on *me*.

She said not a word as we stared each other in the face; but she moved after a little – moved slowly towards the left-hand side of the bed.

The light fell full on her face. A fair, fine woman, with yellowish flaxen hair and light-grey eyes, with a droop in the left eyelid. I noticed these things and fixed them in my mind, before she was quite round at the side of the bed. Without saying a word, without any change in the stony stillness of her face, without any noise following her footfall, she came closer and closer, stopped at the bedhead and lifted the knife to stab me. I laid my arm over my throat to save it; but, as I saw the blow coming, I threw my hand across the bed to the right side, and jerked my body over that way, just as the knife came down within a hair's breadth of my shoulder.

My eyes fixed on her arm and her hand – she gave me time to look at them as she slowly drew the knife out of the bed. A white, well-shaped arm, with a pretty down lying lightly over the fair skin. A delicate lady's hand, with a pink flush round the fingernails.

She drew the knife out, and passed back again slowly to the foot of the bed; she stopped there for a moment looking at me; then she came on without saying a word; without any change in the stony stillness of her face; without any noise following her footfall – came on to the side of the bed where I now lay.

Getting near me, she lifted the knife again, and I drew myself away to the left side. She struck, as before, right into the mattress, with a swift downward action of her arm, and she missed me, as before, by a hair's breadth. This time my eyes wandered from *her* to the knife. It was like the large clasp knives which labouring men use to cut their bread and bacon with. Her delicate little fingers did not hide more than two thirds of the handle; I noticed that it was made of buckhorn, clean and shining as the blade was, and looking like new.

For the second time she drew the knife out of the bed, and suddenly hid it away in the wide sleeve of her gown.

That done, she stopped by the bedside, watching me. For an instant I saw her standing in that position – then the wick of the spent candle fell over into the socket. The flame dwindled to a little blue point, and the room grew dark.

A moment, or less if possible, passed so – and then the wick flamed up, smokily, for the last time. My eyes were still looking for her over the right-hand side of the bed when that last flash of light came. Look as I might, I could see nothing. The woman with the knife was gone.

I began to get back to myself again. I could feel my heart beating; I could hear the woeful moaning of the wind in the wood; I could leap up in bed, and give the alarm before she escaped from the house. "Murder! Wake up there! Murder!"

Nobody answered to the alarm. I rose and groped my way through the darkness to the door of the room. By that way she must have got in. By that way she must have gone out.

The door of the room was fast locked, exactly as I had left it on going to bed!

I looked at the window. Fast locked too!

Hearing a voice outside, I opened the door. There was the landlord, coming towards me along the passage, with his burning candle in one hand and his gun in the other.

"What is it?" he says, looking at me in no very friendly way.

I could only answer him in a whisper. "A woman, with a knife in her hand. In my room. A fair, yellow-haired woman. She jabbed at me with the knife, twice over."

He lifted his candle, and looked at me steadily from head to foot.

"She seems to have missed you twice over."

"I dodged the knife as it came down. It struck the bed each time. Go in and see."

The landlord took his candle into the bedroom immediately. In less than a minute he came out again into the passage in a violent passion.

"The Devil fly away with you and your woman with the knife! There isn't a mark in the bedclothes anywhere. What do you mean by coming into a man's place and frightening his family out of their wits by a dream?"

A dream? The woman who had tried to stab me not a living human being like myself? I began to shake and shiver. The horrors got hold of me at the bare thought of it.

"I'll leave the house," I said. "Better out on the road in the rain and dark than back again in that room, after what I've seen in it. Lend me the light to get my clothes by, and tell me what I'm to pay."

The landlord led the way back with his light into the bedroom. "Pay?" says he. "You'll find your score on the slate when you go downstairs. I wouldn't have taken you in for all the money you've got about you, if I had known your dreaming, screeching ways beforehand. Look at the bed – where's the cut of a knife in it? Look at the window – is the lock bursted? Look at the door (which I heard you fasten yourself) – is it broke in? A murdering woman with a knife in my house! You ought to be ashamed of yourself!"

My eyes followed his hand as it pointed first to the bed – then to the window – then to the door. There was no gainsaying it. The bed sheet was as sound as on the day it was made. The window was fast. The door hung on its hinges as steady as ever. I huddled my clothes on without speaking. We went downstairs together. I looked at the clock in the bar room. The time was twenty minutes past two in the morning. I paid my bill, and the landlord let me out. The rain had ceased, but the night was dark and the wind was bleaker than ever. Little did the darkness, or the cold, or the doubt about the way home matter to *me*. My mind was away from all these things. My mind was fixed on the vision in the bedroom. What had I seen trying to murder me? The creature of a dream? Or that other creature from the world beyond the grave, whom men call ghost? I could make nothing of it as I walked along in the night; I had made nothing of it by midday – when I stood at last, after many times missing my road, on the doorstep of home.

6

MY MOTHER CAME OUT alone to welcome me back. There were no secrets between us two. I told her all that had happened, just as I have told it to you.

She kept silence till I had done. And then she put a question to me.

"What time was it, Francis, when you saw the Woman in your Dream?"

I had looked at the clock when I left the inn, and had noticed that the hands pointed to twenty minutes past two. Allowing for the time consumed in speaking to the landlord and in getting on my clothes, I answered that

I must have first seen the Woman at two o'clock in the morning. In other words, I had not only seen her on my birthday, but at the hour of my birth.

My mother still kept silence. Lost in her own thoughts, she took me by the hand, and led me into the parlour. Her writing desk was on the table by the fireplace. She opened it and signed to me to take a chair by her side.

"My son! Your memory is a bad one, and mine is fast failing me. Tell me again what the woman looked like. I want her to be as well known to both of us, years hence, as she is now."

I obeyed, wondering what strange fancy might be working in her mind. I spoke, and she wrote the words as they fell from my lips:

"Light-grey eyes, with a droop in the left eyelid. Flaxen hair, with a gold-yellow streak in it. White arms, with a down upon them. Little lady's hands, with a rosy-red look about the fingernails."

"Did you notice how she was dressed, Francis?"

"No, Mother."

"Did you notice the knife?"

Yes. A large clasp knife, with a buckhorn handle as good as new."

My mother added the description of the knife. Also the year, month, day of the week and hour of the day when the Dream Woman appeared to me at the inn. That done, she locked up the paper in her desk.

"Not a word, Francis, to your aunt. Not a word to any living soul. Keep your Dream a secret between you and me."

The weeks passed, and the months passed. My mother never returned to the subject again. As for me, time, which wears out all things, wore out my remembrance of the Dream. Little by little, the image of the Woman grew dimmer and dimmer. Little by little, she faded out of my mind.

7

THE STORY OF THE WARNING is now told. Judge for yourself if it was a true warning or a false, when you hear what happened to me on my next birthday.

In the summer time of the year, the Wheel of Fortune turned the right way for me at last. I was smoking my pipe one day, near an old stone quarry at the entrance to our village, when a carriage accident happened, which gave a new turn, as it were, to my lot in life. It was an accident of the commonest kind – not worth mentioning at any length. A lady driving herself; a runaway horse; a cowardly man-servant in attendance, frightened out of his wits; and the stone quarry too near to be agreeable – that is what I saw, all in a few moments, between two whiffs of my pipe. I stopped the horse at the edge of the quarry, and got myself a little hurt by the shaft of the chaise. But that didn't matter. The lady declared I had saved her life, and her husband, coming with her to our cottage the next day, took me into his service then and there. The lady happened to be of a dark complexion, and it may amuse you to hear that my aunt Chance instantly pitched on that circumstance as a means of saving the credit of the cards. Here was the promise of the Queen of Spades performed to the very letter, by means of "a dark woman", just as my aunt had told me! "In the time to come, Francie, beware o' pettin' yer ain blinded intairpretation on the cairds. Ye're ower ready, I trow, to murmur under dispensations of Proavidence that ye canna fathom – like the Eesraelites of auld. I'll say nae mair to ye. Mebbe when the mony's powering into yer poakets, ye'll no forget yer aunt Chance, left like a sparrow on the housetop, wi' a sma' annuitee o' thratty punds a year."

I remained in my situation (at the West End of London) until the spring of the New Year.

About that time, my master's health failed. The doctors ordered him away to foreign parts, and the establishment was broken up. But the turn in my luck still held good. When I left my place, I left it – thanks to the generosity of my kind master – with a yearly allowance granted to me, in remembrance of the day when I had saved my mistress's life. For the future, I could go back to service or not, as I pleased; my little income was enough to support my mother and myself.

My master and mistress left England towards the end of February. Certain matters of business to do for them detained me in London until the last day of the month. I was only able to leave for our village by the evening train, to keep my birthday with my mother as usual. It was bedtime when I got to the cottage, and I was sorry to find that she was far from well. To make matters worse, she had finished her bottle of medicine on the previous day, and had omitted to get it replenished, as the doctor had strictly directed. He dispensed his own medicines, and I offered to go and knock him up. She refused to let me do this and, after giving me my supper, sent me away to my bed.

I fell asleep for a little, and woke again. My mother's bedchamber was next to mine. I heard my aunt Chance's heavy footsteps going to and fro in the room and, suspecting something wrong, knocked at the door. My mother's pains had returned upon her; there was a serious necessity for relieving her sufferings as speedily as possible. I put on my clothes and ran off, with the medicine bottle in my hand, to the other end of the village, where the doctor lived. The church clock chimed the quarter to two on my birthday just as I reached his house. One ring at the night bell brought him to his bedroom window to speak to me. He told me to wait, and he would let me in at the surgery door. I noticed, while I was waiting, that the night was wonderfully fair and warm for the time of year. The old stone quarry where the carriage accident had happened was within view. The moon in the clear heavens lit it up almost as bright as day.

In a minute or two, the doctor let me into the surgery. I closed the door, noticing that he had left his room very lightly clad. He kindly pardoned my mother's neglect of his directions, and set to work at once at compounding the medicine. We were both intent on the bottle – he filling it and I holding the light – when we heard the surgery door suddenly opened from the street.

8

WHO COULD POSSIBLY be up and about in our quiet village at the second hour of the morning? The person who had opened the door appeared within range of the light of the candle. To complete our amazement, the person proved to be a woman!

She walked up to the counter and, standing side by side with me, lifted her veil. At the moment when she showed her face, I heard the church clock strike two. She was a stranger to me, and a stranger to the doctor. She was also, beyond all comparison, the most beautiful woman I have ever seen in my life.

"I saw the light under the door," she said. "I want some medicine."

She spoke quite composedly, as if there was nothing at all extraordinary in her being out in the village at two in the morning and, following me into the surgery to ask for medicine! The doctor stared at her as if he suspected his own eyes of deceiving him. "Who are you?" he asked.

"How do you come to be wandering about at this time in the morning?"

She paid no heed to his questions. She only told him coolly what she wanted.

"I have got a bad toothache. I want a bottle of laudanum."

The doctor recovered himself when she asked for the laudanum. He was on his own ground, you know, when it came to a matter of laudanum, and he spoke to her smartly enough this time.

"Oh, you have got the toothache, have you? Let me look at the tooth."

She shook her head, and laid a two-shilling piece on the counter.

"I won't trouble you to look at the tooth," she said. "There is the money. Let me have the laudanum, if you please."

The doctor put the two-shilling piece back again in her hand.

"I don't sell laudanum to strangers," he answered. "If you are in any distress of body or mind, that is another matter. I shall be glad to help you."

She put the money back in her pocket. "*You* can't help me," she said, as quietly as ever. "Good morning."

With that, she opened the surgery door to go out again into the street.

So far, I had not spoken a word on my side. I had stood with the candle in my hand (not knowing I was holding it) – with my eyes fixed on her, with my mind fixed on her – like a man bewitched. Her looks betrayed, even more plainly than her words, her resolution, in one way or another, to destroy herself. When she opened the door, in my alarm at what might happen I found the use of my tongue.

"Stop!" I cried out. "Wait for me. I want to speak to you before you go away."

She lifted her eyebrows with a look of careless surprise and a mocking smile on her lips.

"What can *you* have to say to me?" She stopped, and laughed to herself. "Why not?" she says. "I have got nothing to do, and nowhere to go." She turned back a step, and nodded to me. "You're a strange man – I think I'll humour you – I'll wait outside." The door of the surgery closed on her. She was gone.

I am ashamed to own what happened next. The only excuse for me is that I was really and truly a man bewitched. I turned me round to follow her out, without once thinking of my mother. The doctor stopped me.

"Don't forget the medicine," he said. "And, if you will take my advice, don't trouble yourself about that woman.

Rouse up the constable. It's his business to look after her – not yours."

I held out my hand for the medicine in silence: I was afraid I should fail in respect if I trusted myself to answer him. He must have seen, as I saw, that she wanted the laudanum to poison herself. He had, to my mind, taken a very heartless view of the matter. I just thanked him when he gave me the medicine – and went out.

She was waiting for me as she had promised; walking slowly to and fro – a tall, graceful, solitary figure in the bright moonbeams. They shed over her fair complexion, her bright golden hair, her large grey eyes, just the light that suited them best. She looked hardly mortal when she first turned to speak to me.

"Well?" she said. "And what do you want?"

In spite of my pride, or my shyness, or my better sense – whichever it might be – all my heart went out to her in a moment. I caught hold of her by the hands, and owned what was in my thoughts, as freely as if I had known her for half a lifetime.

"You mean to destroy yourself," I said. "And I mean to prevent you from doing it. If I follow you about all night, I'll prevent you from doing it."

She laughed. "You saw yourself that he wouldn't sell me the laudanum. Do you really care whether I live or die?" She squeezed my hands gently as she put the question; her eyes searched mine with a languid, lingering look in them that ran through me like fire. My voice died away on my lips; I couldn't answer her.

She understood without my answering. "You have given me a fancy for living, by speaking kindly to me," she said. "Kindness has a wonderful effect on women and dogs, and other domestic animals. It is only men who are superior to kindness. Make your mind easy – I promise to take as much care of myself as if I was the happiest woman living! Don't let me keep you here, out of your bed. Which way are you going?"

Miserable wretch that I was, I had forgotten my mother – with the medicine in my hand!

"I am going home," I said. "Where are you staying? At the inn?"

She laughed her bitter laugh, and pointed to the stone quarry. "There is *my* inn for tonight," she said. "When I got tired of walking about, I rested there."

We walked on together, on my way home. I took the liberty of asking her if she had any friends.

"I thought I had one friend left," she said, "or you would never have met me in this place. It turns out I was wrong. My friend's door was closed in my face some hours since; my friend's servants threatened me with the police. I had nowhere else to go, after trying my luck in your neigh-bourhood, and nothing left but my two-shilling piece and these rags on my back. What respectable innkeeper would take *me* into his house? I walked about, wonder-ing how I could find my way out of the world without disfiguring myself and without suffering much pain. You have no river in these parts. I didn't see my way out of the world till I heard you ringing at the doctor's house. I got a glimpse at the bottles in the surgery, when he let you in, and I thought of the laudanum directly. What were you doing there? Who is that medicine for? Your wife?"

"I am not married."

She laughed again. "Not married! If I was a little better dressed there might be a chance for ME. Where do you live? Here?"

We had arrived, by this time, at my mother's door. She held out her hand to say goodbye. Houseless and homeless as she was, she never asked me to give her a shelter for the night. It was *my* proposal that she should rest under my roof, unknown to my mother and my aunt. Our kitchen was built out at the back of the cottage: she might remain there unseen and unheard until the household was astir in the morning. I led her into the kitchen, and set a chair for her by the dying embers of the fire. I dare say I was to blame – shamefully to blame, if you like. I only wonder what *you* would have done in my place. On your word of honour as a man, would *you* have let that beautiful creature wander back to the shelter of the stone quarry like a stray dog? God help the woman who is foolish enough to trust and love you, if you would have done that!

I left her by the fire, and went to my mother's room.

9

I F YOU HAVE EVER FELT the heartache, you will know what I suffered in secret when my mother took my hand and said, "I am sorry, Francis, that your night's rest has been disturbed through *me*." I gave her the medicine, and I waited by her till the pains abated. My aunt Chance went back to her bed, and my mother and I were left alone. I noticed that her writing desk, moved from its customary place, was on the bed by her side. She saw me looking at it. "This is your birthday, Francis," she said. "Have you anything to tell me?" I had so completely forgotten my Dream that I had no notion of what was passing in her mind when she said those words. For a moment there was a guilty fear in me that she suspected something. I turned away my face and said, "No, mother – I have nothing to tell." She signed to me to stoop down over the pillow and kiss her. "God bless you, my love!" she said. "And many happy returns of the day." She patted my hand and closed her weary eyes and, little by little, fell off peaceably into sleep.

I stole downstairs again. I think the good influence of my mother must have followed me down. At any rate, this is true: I stopped with my hand on the closed kitchen door, and said to myself, "Suppose I leave the house, and leave the village, without seeing her or speaking to her more?"

Should I really have fled from temptation in this way if I had been left to myself to decide? Who can tell? As things were, I was not left to decide. While my doubt was in my mind, she heard me, and opened the kitchen door. My eyes and her eyes met. That ended it.

We were together, unsuspected and undisturbed, for the next two hours. Time enough for her to reveal the secret of her wasted life. Time enough for her to take possession of me as her own, to do with me as she liked. It is needless to dwell here on the misfortunes which had brought her low: they are misfortunes too common to interest anybody.

Her name was Alicia Warlock. She had been born and bred a lady. She had lost her station, her character and her friends. Virtue shuddered at the sight of her, and Vice had got her for the rest of her days. Shocking and common, as I told you. It made no difference to *me*. I have said it already – I say it again – I was a man bewitched. Is there anything so very wonderful in that? Just remember who I was. Among the honest women in my own station in life, where could I have found the like of *her*? Could *they* walk as she walked? And look as she looked? When *they* gave me a kiss, did their lips linger over it as hers did? Had *they* her skin, her laugh, her foot, her hand, her touch? *She* never had a speck of dirt on her: I tell you her flesh was a perfume. When she embraced me, her arms folded round me like the wings of angels, and her smile covered me softly with its light like the sun in heaven. I leave you to laugh at me, or to cry over me, just as your temper may incline. I am not trying to excuse myself – I am trying to explain. You are gentlefolks; what dazzled and maddened *me* is everyday experience to *you*. Fallen or not, angel or devil, it came to this – she was a lady, and I was a groom.

Before the house was astir, I got her away (by the workmen's train) to a large manufacturing town in our parts.

Here – with my savings in money to help her – she could get her outfit of decent clothes, and her lodging among strangers who asked no questions so long as they were paid. Here – now on one pretence and now on another – I could visit her, and we could both plan together what our future lives were to be. I need not tell you that I stood pledged to make her my wife. A man in my station always marries a woman of her sort.

Do you wonder if I was happy at this time? I should have been perfectly happy, but for one little drawback. It was this: I was never quite at my ease in the presence of my promised wife.

I don't mean that I was shy with her, or suspicious of her, or ashamed of her. The uneasiness I am speaking of was caused by a faint doubt in my mind, whether I had not seen her somewhere, before the morning when we met at the doctor's house. Over and over again, I found myself wondering whether her face did not remind me of some other face – *what* other I never could tell. This strange feeling, this one question that could never be answered, vexed me to a degree that you would hardly credit. It came between us at the strangest times – oftenest, however, at night, when the candles were lit. You have known what it is to try and remember a forgotten name – and to fail, search as you may, to find it in your mind. That was my case. I failed to find my lost face, just as you failed to find your lost name.

In three weeks, we had talked matters over, and had arranged how I was to make a clean breast of it at home. By Alicia's advice, I was to describe her as having been one of my fellow servants, during the time when I was employed under my kind master and mistress in London. There was no fear now of my mother taking any harm from the shock of a great surprise. Her health had improved during the three weeks' interval. On the first evening when she was able to take her old place at teatime, I summoned my courage and told her I was going to be married. The poor soul flung her arms round my neck and burst out crying for joy. "Oh, Francis!" she says. "I am so glad you will have somebody to comfort you and care for you when I am gone!" As for my aunt Chance, you can anticipate what *she* did, without being told. Ah, me! If there had really been any prophetic virtue in the cards, what a terrible warning they might have given us that night!

It was arranged that I was to bring my promised wife to dinner at the cottage on the next day.

10

I OWN I WAS PROUD of Alicia when I led her into our little parlour at the appointed time. She had never, to my mind, looked so beautiful as she looked that day. I never noticed any other woman's dress: I noticed hers as carefully as if I had been a woman myself! She wore a black silk gown, with plain collar and cuffs, and a modest lavender-coloured bonnet, with one white rose in it placed at the side. My mother, dressed in her Sunday best, rose up, all in a flutter, to welcome her daughter-in-law that was to be. She walked forward a few steps, half smiling, half in tears – she looked Alicia full in the face – and suddenly stood still. Her cheeks turned white in an instant; her eyes stared in horror; her hands dropped helplessly at her sides. She staggered back, and fell into the arms of my aunt, standing behind her. It was no swoon: she kept her senses. Her eyes turned slowly from Alicia to me. "Francis," she said, "does that woman's face remind you of nothing?"

Before I could answer, she pointed to her writing desk on the table at the fireside. "Bring it!" she cried. "Bring it!"

At the same moment, I felt Alicia's hand laid on my shoulder, and saw Alicia's face red with anger – and no wonder!

"What does this mean?" she asked. "Does your mother want to insult me?"

I said a few words to quiet her; what they were I don't remember – I was so confused and astonished at the time. Before I had done, I heard my mother behind me.

My aunt had fetched her desk. She had opened it; she had taken a paper from it. Step by step, helping herself along by the wall, she came nearer and nearer, with the paper in her hand. She looked at the paper – she looked in Alicia's face – she lifted the long, loose sleeve of her gown and examined her hand and arm. I saw fear suddenly take the place of anger in Alicia's eyes. She shook herself free of my mother's grasp. "Mad!" she said to herself. "And Francis never told me!" With those words she ran out of the room.

I was hastening out after her when my mother signed me to stop. She read the words written on the paper. While they fell slowly, one by one, from her lips, she pointed towards the open door.

"Light-grey eyes, with a droop in the left eyelid. Flaxen hair, with a gold-yellow streak in it. White arms, with a down upon them. Little lady's hand, with a rosy-red look about the fingernails. The Dream Woman, Francis! The Dream Woman!"

Something darkened the parlour window as those words were spoken. I looked sidelong at the shadow. Alicia Warlock had come back! She was peering in at us over the low window blind. There was the fatal face which had first looked at me in the bedroom of the lonely inn! There, resting on the window blind, was the lovely little hand which had held the murderous knife. I *had* seen her before we met in the village. The Dream Woman! The Dream Woman!

11

I EXPECT NOBODY TO APPROVE of what I have next to tell of myself.

In three weeks from the day when my mother had identified her with the Woman of the Dream, I took

Alicia Warlock to church and made her my wife. I was a man bewitched. Again and again I say it, I was a man bewitched!

During the interval before my marriage, our little household at the cottage was broken up. My mother and my aunt quarrelled. My mother, believing in the Dream, entreated me to break off my engagement. My aunt, believing in the cards, urged me to marry.

This difference of opinion produced a dispute between them, in the course of which my aunt Chance – quite unconscious of having any superstitious feelings of her own – actually set out the cards which prophesied happiness to me in my married life, and asked my mother whether anybody but "a blinded heathen could be fule enough, after seeing those cairds, to believe in a dream!" This was, naturally, too much for my mother's patience; hard words followed on either side; Mrs Chance returned in dudgeon to her friends in Scotland. She left me a written statement of my future prospects, as revealed by the cards, and with it an address at which a post-office order would reach her. "The day was no that far off," she remarked, "when Francie might remember what he owed to his aunt

Chance, maintaining her ain unbleemished widowhood on thratty punds a year."

Having refused to give her sanction to my marriage, my mother also refused to be present at the wedding, or to visit Alicia afterwards. There was no anger at the bottom of this conduct on her part. Believing as she did in the Dream, she was simply in mortal fear of my wife. I understood this, and I made allowances for her. Not a cross word passed between us. My one happy remembrance now – though I did disobey her in the matter of my marriage – is this: I loved and respected my good mother to the last.

As for my wife, she expressed no regret at the estrangement between her mother-in-law and herself. By common consent, we never spoke on that subject. We settled in the manufacturing town which I have already mentioned, and we kept a lodging house. My kind master, at my request, granted me a lump sum in place of my annuity. This put us into a good house, decently furnished. For a while, things went well enough. I may describe myself at this time of my life as a happy man.

My misfortunes began with a return of the complaint from which my mother had already suffered. The doctor confessed, when I asked him the question, that there was danger to be dreaded this time. Naturally, after hearing this, I was a good deal away at the cottage. Naturally, also, I left the business of looking after our house, in my absence, to my wife. Little by little, I found her beginning to alter towards me. While my back was turned, she formed acquaintances with people of the doubtful and dissipated sort. One day I observed something in her manner which forced the suspicion on me that she had been drinking. Before the week was out, my suspicion was a certainty. From keeping company with drunkards, she had grown to be a drunkard herself.

I did all a man could do to reclaim her. Quite useless! She had never really returned the love I felt for her: I had no influence, I could do nothing. My mother, hearing of this last worst trouble, resolved to try what her influence could do. Ill as she was, I found her one day dressed to go out.

"I am not long for this world, Francis," she said. "I shall not feel easy on my deathbed unless I have done my best to the last to make you happy. I mean to put my own fears and my own feelings out of the question, and to go with you to your wife, and try what I can do to reclaim her.

Take me home with you, Francis. Let me do all I can to help my son, before it's too late."

How could I disobey her? We took the railway to the town: it was only half an hour's ride. By one o'clock in the afternoon we reached my house. It was our dinner hour, and Alicia was in the kitchen. I was able to take my mother quietly into the parlour, and then prepare my wife for the visit. She had drunk but little at that early hour and, luckily, the devil in her was tamed for the time.

She followed me into the parlour, and the meeting passed off better than I had ventured to forecast; with this one drawback, that my mother – though she tried hard to control herself – shrank from looking my wife in the face when she spoke to her. It was a relief to me when Alicia began to prepare the table for dinner.

She laid the cloth, brought in the bread tray and cut some slices for us from the loaf. Then she returned to the kitchen. At that moment, while I was still anxiously watching my mother, I was startled by seeing the same ghastly change pass over her face which had altered it on the morning when Alicia and she first met. Before I could say a word, she started up with a look of horror.

"Take me back! Home, home again, Francis! Come with me, and never go back more!"

I was afraid to ask for an explanation; I could only sign to her to be silent, and help her quickly to the door. As we passed the bread tray on the table, she stopped and pointed to it.

"Did you see what your wife cut your bread with?" she asked.

"No, Mother; I was not noticing. What was it?"

"Look!"

I did look. A new clasp knife, with a buckhorn handle, lay with the loaf in the bread tray. I stretched out my hand to possess myself of it. At the same moment, there was a noise in the kitchen, and my mother caught me by the arm.

"The knife of the Dream! Francis, I'm faint with fear – take me away before she comes back!"

I couldn't speak, to comfort or even to answer her. Superior as I was to superstition, the discovery of the knife staggered me. In silence, I helped my mother out of the house, and took her home.

I held out my hand to say goodbye. She tried to stop me.

"Don't go back, Francis! Don't go back!"

"I must get the knife, Mother. I must go back by the next train."

I held to that resolution. By the next train I went back.

12

MY WIFE HAD, OF COURSE, discovered our secret departure from the house. She had been drinking. She was in a fury of passion. The dinner in the kitchen was flung under the grate; the cloth was off the parlour table. Where was the knife?

I was foolish enough to ask for it. She refused to give it to me. In the course of the dispute between us which followed, I discovered that there was a horrible story attached to the knife. It had been used in a murder – years since – and had been so skilfully hidden that the authorities had been unable to produce it at the trial. By help of some of her disreputable friends, my wife had been able to purchase this relic of a bygone crime. Her perverted nature set some horrid unacknowledged value on the knife. Seeing there was no hope of getting it by fair means, I determined to search for it, later in the day, in secret. The search was unsuccessful. Night came on, and I left the house to walk about the streets.

You will understand what a broken man I was by this time, when I tell you I was afraid to sleep in the same room with her!

Three weeks passed. Still she refused to give up the knife, and still that fear of sleeping in the same room with her possessed me. I walked about at night, or dozed in the parlour, or sat watching by my mother's bedside. Before the end of the first week in the new month, the worst misfortune of all befell me – my mother died. It wanted then but a short time to my birthday. She had longed to live till that day. I was present at her death. Her last words in this world were addressed to me.

"Don't go back, my son – don't go back!"

I was obliged to go back, if it was only to watch my wife. In the last days of my mother's illness she had spitefully added a sting to my grief by declaring that she would assert her right to attend the funeral. In spite of all that I could do or say, she held to her word. On the day appointed for the burial she forced herself – inflamed and shameless with drink – into my presence, and swore she would walk in the funeral procession to my mother's grave.

This last insult – after all I had gone through already – was more than I could endure. It maddened me. Try to make allowances for a man beside himself. I struck her.

The instant the blow was dealt, I repented it. She crouched down, silent, in a corner of the room, and eyed me steadily. It was a look that cooled my hot blood in an instant. There was no time now to think of making atonement. I could only risk the worst, and make sure of her till the funeral was over. I locked her into her bedroom.

When I came back, after laying my mother in the grave, I found her sitting by the bedside, very much altered in look and bearing, with a bundle on her lap. She faced me quietly; she spoke with a curious stillness in her voice – strangely and unnaturally composed in look and manner.

"No man has ever struck me yet," she said. "My husband shall have no second opportunity. Set the door open, and let me go."

She passed me, and left the room. I saw her walk away up the street.

Was she gone for good?

All that night I watched and waited. No footstep came near the house. The next night, overcome by fatigue, I lay down in bed in my clothes, with the door locked, the key on the table and the candle burning. My slumber was not disturbed. The third night, the fourth, the fifth, the sixth, passed, and nothing happened. I lay down on the seventh night, still suspicious of something happening; still in my clothes; still with the door locked, the key on the table and the candle burning.

My rest was disturbed. I woke twice, without any sensation of uneasiness. The third time, that horrid shivering of the night at the lonely inn, that awful sinking pain at the heart came back again, and roused me in an instant.

My eyes turned towards the left-hand side of the bed. And there stood, looking at me...

The Dream Woman again? No! My wife. The living woman, with the face of the Dream – in the attitude of the Dream – the fair arm up; the knife clasped in the delicate white hand.

I sprang upon her on the instant; but not quickly enough to stop her from hiding the knife. Without a word from me, without a cry from her, I pinioned her in a chair. With one hand I felt up her sleeve; and there, where the Dream Woman had hidden the knife, my wife had hidden it – the knife with the buckhorn handle that looked like new.

What I felt when I made that discovery I could not realize at the time, and I can't describe now. I took one steady look at her with the knife in my hand.

"You meant to kill me?" I said.

"Yes," she answered. "I meant to kill you." She crossed her arms over her bosom, and stared me coolly in the face. "I shall do it yet," she said. "With that knife."

I don't know what possessed me – I swear to you I am no coward – and yet I acted like a coward. The horrors got hold of me. I couldn't look at her – I couldn't speak to her. I left her (with the knife in my hand) and went out into the night.

There was a bleak wind abroad, and the smell of rain was in the air. The church clocks chimed the quarter as I walked beyond the last houses in the town. I asked the first policeman I met what hour that was, of which the quarter past had just struck.

The man looked at his watch, and answered, "Two o'clock." Two in the morning. What day of the month was this day that had just begun? I reckoned it up from the date of my mother's funeral. The horrid parallel between the dream and the reality was complete – it was my birthday!

Had I escaped the mortal peril which the dream fore-told? Or had I only received a second warning?

As that doubt crossed my mind I stopped on my way out of the town. The air had revived me – I felt in some degree like my own self again. After a little thinking, I began to see plainly the mistake I had made in leaving my wife free to go where she liked and to do as she pleased.

I turned instantly, and made my way back to the house.

It was still dark. I had left the candle burning in the bedchamber. When I looked up to the window of the room now, there was no light in it. I advanced to the house door. On going away I remembered to have closed it; on trying it now, I found it open.

I waited outside, never losing sight of the house till daylight. Then I ventured indoors – listened, and heard nothing – looked into the kitchen, scullery, parlour, and found nothing – went up at last into the bedroom. It was empty.

A picklock lay on the floor, which told me how she had gained entrance in the night. And that was the one trace I could find of the Dream Woman.

13

I WAITED IN THE HOUSE till the town was astir for the day, and then I went to consult a lawyer. In the confused state of my mind at the time, I had one clear notion of what I meant to do: I was determined to sell my house and leave the neighbourhood. There were obstacles in the way which I had not counted on. I was told I had creditors to satisfy before I could leave – I, who had given my wife the money to pay my bills regularly every week! Enquiry showed that she had embezzled every farthing of the money that I had entrusted to her. I had no choice but to pay over again.

Placed in this awkward position, my first duty was to set things right, with the help of my lawyer. During my forced sojourn in the town I did two foolish things. And, as a consequence that followed, I heard once more, and heard for the last time, of my wife.

In the first place, having got possession of the knife, I was rash enough to keep it in my pocket. In the second place, having something of importance to say to the lawyer, at a late hour of the evening, I went to his house after dark – alone and on foot. I got there safely enough. Returning, I was seized on from behind by two men, dragged down a dark passage, and robbed – not only of the little money I had about me, but also of the knife. It was the lawyer's opinion (as it was mine) that the thieves were among the disreputable acquaintances formed by my wife, and that they had attacked me at her instigation. To confirm this view I received a letter the next day, without date or address, written in Alicia's hand. The first line informed me that the knife was back again in her possession. The second line reminded me of the day when I had struck her. The third line warned me that she would wash out the stain of that blow in my blood, and repeated the words: "I shall do it with the knife!"

These things happened a year ago. The law laid hands on the men who had robbed me, but from that time to this the law has failed completely to find a trace of my wife.

My story is told. When I had paid the creditors and paid the legal expenses, I had barely five pounds left out of the sale of my house, and I had the world to begin over again. Some months since – drifting here and there – I found my way to Underbridge. The landlord at the inn had known something of my father's family in times past. He gave me (all he had to give) my food, and shelter in the yard. Except on market days, there is nothing to do.

In the coming winter the inn is to be shut up, and I shall have to shift for myself. My old master would help me if I applied to him – but I don't like to apply: he has done more for me already than I deserve. Besides, in another year who knows but my troubles may all be at an end? Next winter will bring me nigh to my next birthday, and my next birthday may be the day of my death. Yes! It's true I sat up all last night, and I heard two in the morning strike – and nothing happened. Still, allowing for that, the time to come is a time I don't trust. My wife has got the knife – my wife is looking for me. I am above superstition, mind! I don't say I believe in dreams; I only say Alicia Warlock is looking for me. It is possible I may be wrong. It is possible I may be right. Who can tell?

The Third Narrative

THE STORY CONTINUED.
BY PERCY FAIRBANK.

14

WE TOOK LEAVE of Francis Raven at the door of Farleigh Hall, with the understanding that he might expect to hear from us again.

The same night Mrs Fairbank and I had a discussion in the sanctuary of our own room. The topic was "The Ostler's Story", and the question in dispute between us turned on the measure of charitable duty that we owed to the ostler himself.

The view I took of the man's narrative was of the purely matter-of-fact kind. Francis Raven had, in my opinion, brooded over the misty connection between his strange dream and his vile wife until his mind was in a state of partial delusion on that subject. I was quite willing to help him with a trifle of money, and to recommend him to the kindness of my lawyer, if he was really in any danger and wanted advice. There my idea of my duty towards this afflicted person began and ended.

Confronted with this sensible view of the matter, Mrs Fairbank's romantic temperament rushed, as usual, into extremes. "I should no more think of losing sight of Francis Raven when his next birthday comes round," says my wife, "than I should think of laying down a good story with the last chapters unread. I am positively determined, Percy, to take him back with us, when we return to France, in the capacity of groom. What does one man more or less among the horses matter to people as rich as we are?" In this strain the partner of my joys and sorrows ran on, perfectly impenetrable to everything that I could say on the side of common sense. Need I tell my married brethren how it ended? Of course I allowed my wife to irritate me, and spoke to her sharply. Of course my wife turned her face away indignantly on the conjugal pillow, and burst into tears. Of course, upon that, "Mr" made his excuses, and "Mrs" had her own way.

Before the week was out we rode over to Underbridge, and duly offered to Francis Raven a place in our service as supernumerary groom.

At first the poor fellow seemed hardly able to realize his own extraordinary good fortune. Recovering himself, he expressed his gratitude modestly and becomingly. Mrs Fairbank's ready sympathies overflowed, as usual, at her lips. She talked to him about our home in France, as if the worn, grey-headed ostler had been a child. "Such a dear old house, Francis – and such pretty gardens! Stables ten times as big as your stables here: quite a choice of rooms for you. You must learn the name of our house – it is called Maison Rouge. Our nearest town is Metz. We are within a walk of the beautiful river Moselle. And when we want a change we have only to take the railway to the frontier, and find ourselves in Germany."

Listening, so far, with a very bewildered face, Francis started and changed colour when my wife reached the end of her last sentence.

"Germany?" he repeated.

"Yes. Does Germany remind you of anything?"

The ostler's eyes looked down sadly on the ground. "Germany reminds me of my wife," he replied.

"Indeed? How?"

"She once told me she had lived in Germany – long before I knew her – in the time when she was a young girl."

"Was she living with relations or friends?"

"She was living as governess in a foreign family."

"In what part of Germany?"

"I don't remember, ma'am. I doubt if she told me."

"Did she tell you the name of the family?"

"Yes, ma'am. It was a foreign name, and it has slipped my memory long since. The head of the family was a wine-grower in a large way of business – I remember that."

"Did you hear what sort of wine he grew? There are wine-growers in our neighbourhood. Was it Moselle wine?"

"I couldn't say, ma'am. I doubt if I ever heard."

There the conversation dropped. We engaged to communicate with Francis Raven before we left England, and took our leave.

I had made my arrangements to pay our round of visits to English friends, and to return to Maison Rouge in the summer. On the eve of departure, certain difficulties in connection with the management of some landed property of mine in Ireland obliged us to alter our plans. Instead of getting back to our house in France in the summer, we only returned a week or two before

Christmas. Francis Raven accompanied us, and was duly established, in the nominal capacity of stable helper, among the servants at Maison Rouge.

Before long, some of the objections to taking him into our employment, which I had foreseen and had vainly mentioned to my wife, forced themselves on our attention in no very agreeable form.

Francis Raven failed (as I had feared he would) to get on smoothly with his fellow servants. They were all French, and not one of them understood English. Francis, on his side, was equally ignorant of French. His reserved manners, his melancholy temperament, his solitary ways – all told against him. Our servants called him "the English Bear". He grew widely known in the neighbourhood under his nickname. Quarrels took place, ending once or twice in blows. It became plain, even to Mrs Fairbank herself, that some wise change must be made. While we were still considering what the change was to be, the unfortunate ostler was thrown on our hands for some time to come by an accident in the stables. Still pursued by his proverbial ill luck, the poor wretch's leg was broken by a kick from a horse.

He was attended to by our own surgeon, in his comfortable bedroom at the stables. As the date of his birthday drew near he was still confined to his bed.

Physically speaking, he was doing very well. Morally speaking, the surgeon was not satisfied. Francis Raven was suffering under some unacknowledged mental disturbance, which interfered seriously with his rest at night. Hearing this, I thought it my duty to tell the medical attendant what was preying on the patient's mind. As a practical man, he shared my opinion that the ostler was in a state of delusion on the subject of his Wife and his Dream. "Curable delusion, in my opinion," the surgeon added, "if the experiment could be fairly tried."

"How can it be tried?" I asked.

Instead of replying, the surgeon put a question to me, on his side.

"Do you happen to know," he said, "that this year is leap year?"

"Mrs Fairbank reminded me of it yesterday," I answered. "Otherwise I might *not* have known it."

"Do you think Francis Raven knows that this year is leap year?"

(I began to see dimly what my friend was driving at.)

"It depends," I answered, "on whether he has got an English almanac. Suppose he has *not* got the almanac – what then?"

"In that case," pursued the surgeon, "Francis Raven is innocent of all suspicion that there is a twenty-ninth day in February this year. As a necessary consequence – what will he do? He will anticipate the appearance of the Woman with the Knife at two in the morning on the twenty-ninth of February, instead of the first of March. Let him suffer all his superstitious terrors on the wrong day. Leave him, on the day that is really his birthday, to pass a perfectly quiet night, and to be as sound asleep as other people at two in the morning. And then, when he wakes comfortably in time for his breakfast, shame him out of his delusion by telling him the truth."

I agreed to try the experiment. Leaving the surgeon to caution Mrs Fairbank on the subject of leap year, I went to the stables to see Francis Raven.

15

THE POOR FELLOW was full of forebodings of the fate in store for him on the ominous first of March. He eagerly entreated me to order one of the menservants to sit up with him on the birthday morning. In granting his request, I asked him to tell me on which day of the week his birthday fell. He reckoned the days on his fingers, and proved his innocence of all suspicion that it was leap year by fixing on the twenty-ninth of February, in the full persuasion that it was the first of March. Pledged to try the surgeon's experiment, I left his error uncorrected, of course. In so doing, I took my first step blindfold towards the last act in the drama of the Ostler's Dream.

The next day brought with it a little domestic difficulty, which indirectly and strangely associated itself with the coming end.

My wife received a letter, inviting us to assist in celebrating the "Silver Wedding" of two worthy German neighbours of ours – Mr and Mrs Beldheimer. Mr Beldheimer was a large wine-grower on the banks of the Moselle. His house was situated on the frontier line of France and Germany, and the distance from our house was sufficiently considerable to make it necessary for us to sleep under our host's roof. Under these circumstances, if we accepted the invitation, a comparison of dates showed that we should be away from home on the morning of the first of March. Mrs Fairbank – holding to her absurd resolution to see with her own eyes what might, or might not, happen to Francis Raven on his birthday – flatly declined to leave Maison Rouge. "It's easy to send an excuse," she said, in her offhand manner.

I failed, for my part, to see any easy way out of the difficulty. The celebration of a "Silver Wedding" in Germany is the celebration of twenty-five years of happy married life, and the host's claim upon the consideration of his friends on such an occasion is something in the nature of a royal "command". After considerable discussion, finding my wife's obstinacy invincible, and feeling that the absence of both of us from the festival would certainly offend our friends, I left Mrs Fairbank to make her excuses for herself, and directed her to accept the invitation so far as I was concerned. In so doing, I took my second step, blindfold, towards the last act in the drama of the Ostler's Dream.

A week elapsed; the last days of February were at hand. Another domestic difficulty happened, and again, this event also proved to be strangely associated with the coming end.

My head groom at the stables was one Joseph Rigobert. He was an ill-conditioned fellow, inordinately vain of his personal appearance, and by no means scrupulous in his conduct with women. His one virtue consisted in his fondness for horses, and in the care he took of the animals under his charge. In a word, he was too good a groom to be easily replaced, or he would have quitted my service long since. On the occasion of which I am now writing, he was reported to me by my steward as growing idle and disorderly in his habits. The principal offence alleged against him was that he had been seen that day in the city of Metz, in the company of a woman (supposed to be an Englishwoman), whom he was entertaining at a tavern, when he ought to have been on his way back to Maison Rouge. The man's defence was that "the lady" (as he called her) was an English stranger, unacquainted with the ways of the place, and that he had only shown her where she could obtain some refreshment, at her own request. I administered the necessary reprimand, without troubling myself to enquire further into the matter. In failing to do this, I took my third step, blindfold, towards the last act in the drama of the Ostler's Dream.

On the evening of the twenty-eighth, I informed the servants at the stables that one of them must watch through the night by the Englishman's bedside. Joseph Rigobert immediately volunteered for the duty – as a means, no doubt, of winning his way back to my favour. I accepted his proposal.

That day, the surgeon dined with us. Towards midnight he and I left the smoking room, and repaired to Francis Raven's bedside. Rigobert was at his post, with no very agreeable expression on his face. The Frenchman and the Englishman had evidently not got on well together so far. Francis Raven lay helpless on his bed, waiting silently for two in the morning, and the Dream Woman.

"I have come, Francis, to bid you goodnight," I said, cheerfully. "Tomorrow morning I shall look in at breakfast time, before I leave home on a journey."

"Thank you for all your kindness, sir. You will not see me alive tomorrow morning. She will find me this time. Mark my words – she will find me this time."

"My good fellow! She couldn't find you in England. How in the world is she to find you in France?"

"It's borne in on my mind, sir, that she will find me here. At two in the morning on my birthday I shall see her again, and see her for the last time."

"Do you mean that she will kill you?"

"I mean that, sir. She will kill me – with the knife."

"And with Rigobert in the room to protect you?"

"I am a doomed man. Fifty Rigoberts couldn't protect me."

"And yet you wanted somebody to sit up with you?"

"Mere weakness, sir. I don't like to be left alone on my deathbed."

I looked at the surgeon. If he had encouraged me, I should certainly, out of sheer compassion, have confessed to Francis Raven the trick that we were playing him. The surgeon held to his experiment; the surgeon's face plainly said – No."

The next day (the twenty-ninth of February) was the day of the "Silver Wedding". The first thing in the morning, I went to Francis Raven's room. Rigobert met me at the door.

"How has he passed the night?" I asked.

"Saying his prayers, and looking for ghosts," Rigobert answered. "A lunatic asylum is the only proper place for him."

I approached the bedside. "Well, Francis, here you are, safe and sound, in spite of what you said to me last night."

His eyes rested on mine with a vacant, wondering look.

"I don't understand it," he said.

"Did you see anything of your wife when the clock struck two?"

"No, sir."

"Did anything happen?"

"Nothing happened, sir."

"Doesn't *this* satisfy you that you were wrong?"

His eyes still kept their vacant, wondering look. He only repeated the words he had spoken already:

"I don't understand it."

I made a last attempt to cheer him. "Come, come, Francis! Keep a good heart. You will be out of bed in a fortnight."

He shook his head on the pillow. "There's something wrong," he said. "I don't expect you to believe me, sir. I only say, there's something wrong – and time will show it."

I left the room. Half an hour later I started for Mr Beldheimer's house; leaving the arrangements for the morning of the first of March in the hands of the doctor and my wife.

16

THE ONE THING WHICH principally struck me when I joined the guests at the "Silver Wedding" is also the one thing which it is necessary to mention here. On this joyful occasion a noticeable lady present was out of spirits. That lady was no other than the heroine of the festival, the mistress of the house!

In the course of the evening I spoke to Mr Beldheimer's eldest son on the subject of his mother. As an old friend of the family, I had a claim on his confidence which the young man willingly recognized.

"We have had a very disagreeable matter to deal with," he said, "and my mother has not recovered the painful impression left on her mind. Many years since, when my sisters were children, we had an English governess in the house. She left us, as we then understood, to be married. We heard no more of her until a week or ten days since, when my mother received a letter, in which our ex-governess described herself as being in a condition of great poverty and distress. After much hesitation she had ventured – at the suggestion of a lady who had been kind to her – to write to her former employers, and to appeal to their remembrance of old times. You know my mother:

she is not only the most kind-hearted, but the most innocent of women – it is impossible to persuade her of the
wickedness that there is in the world. She replied by return
of post, inviting the governess to come here and see her,
and enclosing the money for her travelling expenses. When
my father came home, and heard what had been done, he
wrote at once to his agent in London to make enquiries,
enclosing the address on the governess's letter. Before he
could receive the agent's reply the governess arrived. She
produced the worst possible impression on his mind. The
agent's letter, arriving a few days later, confirmed his sus-
picions. Since we had lost sight of her, the woman had led
a most disreputable life. My father spoke to her privately:
he offered – on condition of her leaving the house – a sum
of money to take her back to England. If she refused, the
alternative would be an appeal to the authorities and a
public scandal. She accepted the money, and left the house.
On her way back to England she appears to have stopped
at Metz. You will understand what sort of woman she is,
when I tell you that she was seen the other day in a tavern
with your handsome groom, Joseph Rigobert."

While my informant was relating these circumstances,
my memory was at work. I recalled what Francis Raven

had vaguely told us of his wife's experience in former days, as governess in a German family. A suspicion of the truth suddenly flashed across my mind.

"What was the woman's name?" I asked.

Mr Beldheimer's son answered:

"Alicia Warlock."

I had but one idea when I heard that reply – to get back to my house without a moment's needless delay. It was then ten o'clock at night – the last train to Metz had left long since. I arranged with my young friend – after duly informing him of the circumstances – that I should go by the first train in the morning, instead of staying to breakfast with the other guests who slept in the house.

At intervals during the night I wondered uneasily how things were going on at Maison Rouge. Again and again, the same question occurred to me, on my journey home in the early morning – the morning of the first of March. As the event proved, but one person in my house knew what really happened at the stables on Francis Raven's birthday. Let Joseph Rigobert take my place as narrator, and tell the story of the end to you – as he told it, in times past, to his lawyer and to me.

Fourth (and Last) Narrative

RESPECTED SIR – on the twenty-seventh of February
I was sent, on business connected with the stables at
Maison Rouge, to the city of Metz. On the public promenade
I met a magnificent woman. Complexion blonde. Nationality,
English. We mutually admired each other; we fell into con-
versation. (She spoke French perfectly – with the English
accent.) I offered refreshment; my proposal was accepted.
We had a long and interesting interview – we discovered
that we were made for each other. So far, who is to blame?

Is it my fault that I am a handsome man – universally
agreeable, as such, to the fair sex? Is it a criminal offence
to be accessible to the amiable weakness of love? I ask
again, who is to blame? Clearly, Nature. Not the beautiful
lady – not my humble self.

To resume. The most hard-hearted person living
will understand that two beings made for each other

could not possibly part without an appointment to meet again.

I made arrangements for the accommodation of the lady in the village near Maison Rouge. She consented to honour me with her company at supper, in my apartment at the stables, on the night of the twenty-ninth. The time fixed on was the time when the other servants were accustomed to retire – eleven o'clock.

Among the grooms attached to the stables was an Englishman, laid up with a broken leg. His name was Francis. His manners were repulsive; he was ignorant of the French language. In the kitchen he went by the nickname of "the English Bear". Strange to say, he was a great favourite with my master and my mistress. They even humoured certain superstitious terrors to which this repulsive person was subject – terrors into the nature of which I, as an advanced freethinker, never thought it worth my while to enquire.

On the evening of the twenty-eighth, the Englishman, being a prey to the terrors which I have mentioned, requested that one of his fellow servants might sit up with him for that night only. The wish that he expressed was backed by Mr Fairbank's authority. Having already incurred my master's displeasure – in what way, a proper sense of my own dignity forbids me to relate – I volunteered to watch by the bedside of the English Bear. My object was to satisfy Mr Fairbank that I bore no malice, on my side, after what had occurred between us. The wretched Englishman passed a night of delirium. Not understanding his barbarous language, I could only gather from his gestures that he was in deadly fear of some fancied apparition at his bedside. From time to time, when this madman disturbed my slumbers, I quieted him by swearing at him. This is the shortest and best way of dealing with persons in his condition.

On the morning of the twenty-ninth, Mr Fairbank left us on a journey.

Later in the day, to my unspeakable disgust, I found that I had not done with the Englishman yet. In Mr Fairbank's absence, Mrs Fairbank took an incomprehensible interest in the question of my delirious fellow servant's repose at night. Again, one or other of us was to watch by his bedside, and to report it, if anything happened. Expecting my fair friend to supper, it was necessary to make sure that the other servants at the stables would be safe in their beds that night. Accordingly, I volunteered once more to be the man who kept watch. Mrs Fairbank complimented me on my humanity. I possess great command over my feelings. I accepted the compliment without a blush.

Twice, after nightfall, my mistress and the doctor (this last staying in the house, in Mr Fairbank's absence) came to make enquiries. Once, *before* the arrival of my fair friend – and once *after*. On the second occasion (my apartment being next door to the Englishman's), I was obliged to hide my charming guest in the harness room. She consented, with angelic resignation, to immolate her dignity to the servile necessities of my position. A more amiable woman (so far) I never met with!

After the second visit I was left free. It was then close on midnight. Up to that time, there was nothing in the behaviour of the mad Englishman to reward Mrs Fairbank and the doctor for presenting themselves at his bedside. He lay half awake, half asleep, with an odd, wondering kind of look in his face. My mistress at parting warned me to be particularly watchful of him towards two in the morning. The doctor (in case anything happened) left me a large handbell to ring, which could easily be heard at the house.

Restored to the society of my fair friend, I spread the supper table. A pâté, a sausage and a few bottles of generous Moselle wine composed our simple meal. When persons adore each other, the intoxicating illusion of Love transforms the simplest meal into a banquet. With immeasurable capacities for enjoyment, we sat down to table. At the very moment when I placed my fascinating companion in a chair, the infamous Englishman in the next room took that occasion, of all others, to become restless and noisy once more. He struck with his stick on the floor; he cried out, in a delirious access of terror, "Rigobert! Rigobert!"

The sound of that lamentable voice, suddenly assailing our ears, terrified my fair friend. She lost all her charming colour in an instant. "Good Heavens!" she exclaimed. "Who is that in the next room?"

"A mad Englishman."

"An Englishman?"

"Compose yourself, my angel. I will quiet him."

The lamentable voice called out on me again, "Rigobert! Rigobert!"

My fair friend caught me by the arm. "Who is he? What is his name?"

Something in her face struck me as she put that question. A spasm of jealousy shook me to the soul. "You know him?" I said.

"His name!" she vehemently repeated. "His name!"

"Francis," I answered.

"Francis – *what*?"

I shrugged my shoulders. I could neither remember nor pronounce the barbarous English surname. I could only tell her it began with an R.

She dropped back into the chair. Was she going to faint? No, she recovered, and more than recovered, her lost colour. Her eyes flashed superbly. What did it mean? Profoundly as I understand women in general, I was puzzled by *this* woman!

"You know him?" I repeated.

She laughed at me. "What nonsense! How should I know him? Go and quiet the wretch."

My looking glass was near. One glance at it satisfied me that no woman in her senses could prefer the Englishman to me. I recovered my self-respect. I hastened to the Englishman's bedside.

The moment I appeared he pointed eagerly towards my room. He overwhelmed me with a torrent of words in his own language. I made out, from his gestures and his looks, that he had, in some incomprehensible manner, discovered the presence of my guest; and, stranger still, that he was scared by the idea of a person in my room. I endeavoured to compose him on the system which I have already mentioned – that is to say, I swore at him in *my* language. The result not proving satisfactory, I own I shook my fist in his face, and left the bedchamber.

Returning to my fair friend, I found her walking backwards and forwards in a state of excitement wonderful to behold. She had not waited for me to fill her glass – she had begun the generous Moselle in my absence. I prevailed on her with difficulty to place herself at the table. Nothing would induce her to eat. "My appetite is gone," she said. "Give me wine."

The generous Moselle deserves its name – delicate on the palate, with prodigious "body". The strength of this fine wine produced no stupefying effect on my remarkable guest. It appeared to strengthen and exhilarate her – nothing more. She always spoke in the same low tone, and always, turn the conversation as I might, brought it back with the same dexterity to the subject of the Englishman in the next room. In any other woman this persistency would have offended me. My lovely guest was irresistible; I answered her questions with the docility of a child. She possessed all the amusing eccentricity of her nation. When I told her of the accident which confined the Englishman to his bed, she sprang to her feet. An extraordinary smile irradiated her countenance. She said, "Show me the horse who broke his leg! I must, and will, see that horse!" I took her down to the stables. She kissed the horse – on my word of honour, she kissed the horse! That struck me. I said, "You *do* know the man – and he has wronged you in some way." No! She would not admit it, even then. "I kiss all beautiful animals," she said. "Haven't I kissed *you*?" With that charming explanation of her conduct, she ran back up the stairs. I only remained behind to lock the stable door again. When I rejoined her, I made a startling discovery. I caught her coming out of the Englishman's room.

"I was just going downstairs again to call you," she said. "The man in there is getting noisy once more."

The mad Englishman's voice assailed our ears again.

"Rigobert! Rigobert!"

He was a frightful object to look at when I saw him this time. His eyes were staring wildly; the perspiration was pouring over his face. In a panic of terror he clasped his hands; he pointed up to heaven. By every sign and gesture that a man can make, he entreated me not to leave him again. I really could not help smiling. The idea of my staying with *him*, and leaving my fair friend by herself in the next room!

I turned to the door. When the mad wretch saw me leaving him he burst out into a screech of despair – so shrill that I feared it might awaken the sleeping servants.

My presence of mind in emergencies is proverbial among those who know me. I tore open the cupboard in which he kept his linen – seized a handful of his handkerchiefs – gagged him with one of them, and secured his hands with the others. There was now no danger of his alarming the servants. After tying the last knot, I looked up.

The door between the Englishman's room and mine was open. My fair friend was standing on the threshold – watching *him* as he lay helpless on the bed; watching *me* as I tied the last knot.

"What are you doing there?" I asked. "Why did you open the door?"

She stepped up to me, and whispered her answer in my ear, with her eyes all the time upon the man on the bed.

"I heard him scream."

"Well?"

"I thought you had killed him."

I drew back from her in horror. The suspicion of me which her words implied was sufficiently detestable in itself. But her manner when she uttered the words was more revolting still. It so powerfully affected me that I started back from that beautiful creature, as I might have recoiled from a reptile crawling over my flesh.

Before I had recovered myself sufficiently to reply, my nerves were assailed by another shock. I suddenly heard my mistress's voice, calling to me from the stable yard.

There was no time to think – there was only time to act. The one thing needed was to keep Mrs Fairbank from ascending the stairs, and discovering – not my lady guest only – but the Englishman also, gagged and bound on his bed. I instantly hurried to the yard. As I ran down the stairs I heard the stable clock strike the quarter to two in the morning.

My mistress was eager and agitated. The doctor (in attendance on her) was smiling to himself, like a man amused at his own thoughts.

"Is Francis awake or asleep?" Mrs Fairbank enquired.

"He has been a little restless, madam. But he is now quiet again. If he is not disturbed" (I added those words to prevent her from ascending the stairs) "he will soon fall off into a quiet sleep."

"Has nothing happened since I was here last?"

"Nothing, madam."

The doctor lifted his eyebrows with a comical look of distress.

"Alas, alas, Mrs Fairbank!" he said. "Nothing has happened! The days of romance are over!"

"It is not two o'clock yet," my mistress answered, a little irritably.

The smell of the stables was strong on the morning air. She put her handkerchief to her nose and led the way out of the yard, by the north entrance – the entrance communicating with the gardens and the house. I was ordered to follow her, along with the doctor. Once out of the smell of the stables, she began to question me again. She was unwilling to believe that nothing had occurred in her absence. I invented the best answers I could think of on the spur of the moment, and the doctor stood by, laughing. So the minutes passed, till the clock struck two. Upon that, Mrs Fairbank announced her intention of personally visiting the Englishman in his room. To my great relief, the doctor interfered to stop her from doing this.

"You have heard that Francis is just falling asleep," he said. "If you enter his room you may disturb him. It is essential to the success of my experiment that he should have a good night's rest, and that he should own it himself, before I tell him the truth. I must request, madam, that you will not disturb the man. Rigobert will ring if anything happens."

My mistress was unwilling to yield. For the next five minutes at least, there was a warm discussion between the two. In the end, Mrs Fairbank was obliged to give way – for the time. "In half an hour," she said, "Francis will either be sound asleep, or awake again. In half an hour I shall come back." She took the doctor's arm. They returned together to the house.

Left by myself, with half an hour before me, I resolved to take the Englishwoman back to the village – then, returning to the stables, to remove the gag and the bindings from Francis, and to let him screech to his heart's content. What would his alarming the whole establishment matter to *me*, after I had got rid of the compromising presence of my guest?

Returning to the yard I heard a sound like the creaking of an open door on its hinges. The gate of the north entrance I had just closed with my own hand. I went round to the west entrance at the back of the stables. It opened on a field crossed by two footpaths in Mr Fairbank's grounds. The nearest footpath led to the village. The other led to the high road and the river.

Arriving at the west entrance I found the door open – swinging to and fro slowly in the fresh morning breeze. I had myself locked and bolted that door after admitting my fair friend at eleven o'clock. A vague dread of something wrong stole its way into my mind. I hurried back to the stables.

I looked into my own room. It was empty. I went to the harness room. Not a sign of the woman was there. I returned to my room, and approached the door of the Englishman's bedchamber. Was it possible that she had remained there during my absence? An unaccountable reluctance to open the door made me hesitate, with my hand on the lock. I listened. There was not a sound inside. I called softly. There was no answer. I drew back a step, still hesitating. I noticed something dark, moving slowly in the crevice between the bottom of the door and the boarded floor. Snatching up the candle from the table, I held it low, and looked. The dark, slowly moving object was a stream of blood!

That horrid sight roused me. I opened the door.

The Englishman lay on his bed – alone in the room. He was stabbed in two places – in the throat and in the heart. The weapon was left in the second wound. It was a knife of English manufacture, with a handle of buckhorn as good as new.

I instantly gave the alarm. Witnesses can speak to what followed. It is monstrous to suppose that I am guilty of the murder. I admit that I am capable of committing follies, but I shrink from the bare idea of a crime. Besides, I had no motive for killing the man. The woman murdered him in my absence. The woman escaped by the west entrance while I was talking to my mistress. I have no more to say. I swear to you what I have here written is a true statement of all that happened on the morning of the first of March.

Accept, sir, the assurance of my sentiments of profound gratitude and respect.

– Joseph Rigobert

Last Lines

ADDED BY
PERCY FAIRBANK

T RIED FOR THE MURDER of Francis Raven, Joseph Rigobert was found not guilty; the papers of the assassinated man presenting ample evidence of the deadly animosity felt towards him by his wife.

The investigations pursued on the morning when the crime was committed showed that the murderess, after leaving the stable, had taken the footpath which led to the river. The river was dragged – without result. It remains doubtful to this day whether she died by drowning or not. The one thing certain is that Alicia Warlock was never seen again.

So – beginning in mystery, ending in mystery – the Dream Woman passes from your view. Ghost, demon or living human creature – say for yourselves which she is. Or, knowing what unfathomed wonders are around you, what unfathomed wonders are *in* you, let the wise words of the greatest of all poets be explanation enough:

> We are such stuff
> As dreams are made on, and our little life
> Is rounded with a sleep.

Note on the Text

The text in this edition is based on the expanded version published in *The Frozen Deep and Other Stories* (1874). The spelling and punctuation have been standardized, modernized and made consistent throughout.

Extra Material

on

Wilkie Collins's

The Dream Woman

Wilkie Collins's Life

William Wilkie Collins was born on 8th January 1824. His
middle name derived from his godfather, the renowned
Scottish artist David Wilkie, and he was known for most of
his life by this middle name, to avoid confusion with his father
William. Wilkie was the first child of a happy and secure
marriage: his mother had worked as a teacher, governess and
actress, while his father was a renowned painter, who once
sold a painting to the Prince Regent for 150 guineas. William
knew the Wordsworths, regularly received the Coleridges in his
house and painted Coleridge's daughter Sara. He was elected
to the Royal Academy in 1820. Both parents were Tory High
Anglicans, though Wilkie never shared either their religious
or political beliefs. In his later years, William suffered severe
distress from "rheumatic gout", and this complaint chronically
affected Wilkie too in later life, leading to the surmise that –
whatever this ailment actually was, and theories have varied
– there may well have been a genetic disposition in the family
towards the condition, and towards ill health in general.

Wilkie was born in the St Marylebone district of London,
and spent much of his life within the vicinity of the central
London thoroughfare of Oxford Street. Commentators have
speculated as to whether his birth may have been slightly
difficult, since he had a very large head in proportion to his
body, with a slight indentation on one side and a protuberance
on the other, and very short arms and legs. As an adult he was
only 5' 6" tall.

His parents encouraged their children to read and to paint,
and from his infancy Wilkie was reading *Don Quixote*, *The
Vicar of Wakefield*, *The Arabian Nights* and the novels of
Walter Scott, which he retained a high regard for throughout

his life. His parents undertook extensive rambles in outlying areas of Britain, including a four-month stay in Wales; they brought Wilkie along with them, and these trips further stimulated his imagination. At the age of eleven, he attended a day school near his parents' house for a short period, but in 1836 went with them and his younger brother Charles to Italy, where the family spent two years. This extended residence abroad, with its exposure to a different cuisine, language, morality, religion and world view, was crucial for Wilkie's development as a writer. He had Italian lessons, painted, went to art galleries and explored his surroundings. His parents held back from fraternizing too much with the locals, whom they saw as idolatrous heathens, but Wilkie mixed freely with the Italian children and ended up speaking the language fluently. On the family's return to London in August 1838, he started attending a boarding school in Highbury, a mile north-east of central London. His artistic family background and time spent abroad set him apart from his fellow pupils, as did his physical appearance. However, according to his own account, he managed to escape bullying from the older boys by inventing an enthralling tale every night, like Scheherazade in *The Arabian Nights*. He later claimed that it was this which first awakened his facility as a weaver of stories.

Work and Early Writings   Wilkie remained at this school till he was seventeen, when his father obtained a job for him as a clerk at a tea-importer's office. This may have been an attempt on his father's side to coax Wilkie into a more practical life than that of a writer. William may even have subsidized the wages the firm paid to Wilkie, for his son seems to have been able to take long holidays whenever he wanted to, and the duties, although extremely boring, were not too onerous – Wilkie spent most of his time churning out novels, plays and poetry, none of which were published or have survived, and which he later termed "the usual literary rubbish". He spent five years in this office, and although he found it tedious, he never expressed a desire to go to university. His father tried to persuade him to enter the civil service and the admiralty, but with no success. In Wilkie's third novel *Hide and Seek* (1854), one of the characters – a young man working as a clerk in a tea-importer's – states: "They all say it's a good opening for me, and talk about the respectability of commercial pursuits; I don't want to be respectable, and I hate commercial pursuits."

In 1842 William and the eighteen-year-old Wilkie undertook an extensive tour of Scotland and the Shetland Islands. The scenery made a profound impact on Wilkie, which he would remember for the rest of his life.

His first publication was the short story *The Last Stage* *First Publications* *Coachman*, which appeared in 1843 in *The Illuminated Magazine*, although it appears that he had had other pieces published anonymously around this time in the numerous literary journals of the period.

In August 1844, Wilkie went abroad for the first time without his parents, but with a young family friend of his own age. In France he commented approvingly on the food, but was apparently somewhat critical of what he termed the surrounding "dissipation". This seems rather strange, considering his own dislike of orthodox conventions, but it is possible that this disapproval was a front put on by the two men to cover up their own misbehaviour.

Back home, he started writing his first novel in October, *Iolâni*, set in Tahiti before it was discovered by Europeans and Christianized. He submitted the manuscript to various publishers in 1845, but it was rejected by all of them. The explicit scenes of unbridled licentiousness among the indigenous population may have scared off publishers at this time of Victorian Christian morality.

In 1846, his father entered Wilkie for the Bar. While undergoing his first year's legal training, he started his second novel, *Antonina*. It was set in ancient Rome, and already some of the dramatic themes of the author's later works are apparent, such as brothers separated in childhood, abnormal mental states and criticism of religious fanaticism.

He had written about half of it when his father died in *Death of His Father* February 1847. He abandoned work on the novel temporarily, and over the next few months wrote the lucid and warm biography of his father, *Memoirs of the Life of William Collins, Esq., R.A.* It was published by Longmans in November 1848, received excellent reviews and sold extremely well. However, his father had left all his income in trust to his widow, so Wilkie and his brother were still no better off financially.

After Willliam's death, the Collins house became the meeting place of a large set of young artists, literati and intellectuals, including members of the burgeoning Pre-Raphaelite Brotherhood. They put on theatricals at their various residences, and

Wilkie, who always had an interest in drama, began his stage career by adapting French melodramas.

He also kept up his painting, and in 1849 had a picture exhibited at the Royal Academy Summer Exhibition – his only success in this field. He gradually relinquished graphic art and devoted himself to literature, although his brother Charles tried, without much success, to follow the path of his father and establish a career as a painter, mainly in the Pre-Raphaelite mode.

Antonina was published in early 1850 and, despite its melodramatic and absurd plot, received excellent reviews, including one that compared the author to Shakespeare, and another that placed him in the "first rank" of English novelists.

During the summer vacation from his legal studies in the same year, he undertook an extended tour of Cornwall and the West Country, and then wrote an excellent, highly informative travel guide of the area, entitled *Rambles Beyond Railways*, which appeared in 1851.

Bentley, the London publisher who had produced *Antonina*, also issued a highly respected literary journal, *Bentley's Miscellany*, and over the next two years, Collins published several short stories, articles and reviews in this magazine.

Relationship with Dickens In March 1851, Collins met Charles Dickens for the first time at the house of a mutual acquaintance. The indefatigable older author (he was twelve years senior to Collins) was at that time staging plays both in London and the provinces in aid of his newly established Guild of Literature and Art, and he invited Collins to act in some of his productions. They quickly struck up a friendship, and roamed London together gathering materials and impressions for their work. Wilkie was at this time contributing articles not only to Bentley's publication, but also to the radical magazine *The Leader*, for which he penned a series of articles on hypnotism and mesmerism.

He passed his final law exams and was called to the Bar in 1852. However, although his knowledge of the law provided him with valuable material for some of his intricate plots, he never worked in the profession. Immediately upon graduation, he joined Dickens's acting troupe on an extremely successful tour of Britain. In 1852 he made his first contribution to *Household Words*, the weekly journal which Dickens had recently launched and now edited. This was the novella *A Terribly Strange Bed*. He also published a short novel, *Mr*

Wray's Cash Box, in January of the same year – this effort was his only foray into the field of Dickensian Christmas short stories.

In November 1852, Bentley published Wilkie's next novel, *Basil*. The work has a lurid subject matter, and has been described as one of the first "sensation novels", a genre which was to become hugely popular with the newly literate masses, and which was generally at odds with the prevailing Victorian morality. Although most of Collins's literary friends were extremely approving, the reviews – while generally praising the high quality of the writing – deplored what one journal called the book's "vicious atmosphere".

Reports of Collins at this time described him as a brilliant conversationalist, and very charming towards women. He continued to contribute short stories, articles and reviews, both to *Household Words* and other literary periodicals of the time.

In October to December of 1853, Dickens, Collins and *Travels with Dickens* the artist Augustus Egg travelled to the Continent, taking in *and Illness* impressions of France, Switzerland and Italy. In June 1854, Collins's next novel, *Hide and Seek*, was published. It was praised highly for its economy of style, and was described in one magazine as "a work which everyone should read".

In early 1855, he went on another holiday with Dickens to Paris, and it was during these trips abroad that the first signs appeared of the condition he later called "rheumatic gout", which became progressively worse throughout his life. The symptoms included neuralgia and shivering. It has been speculated that the physical condition was a belated after-effect of a venereal disease which Wilkie may have caught earlier in life.

In early 1856 he published *After Dark*, a selection of his earlier short stories, and then spent another six weeks in Paris with Dickens and his family, where he was once again ill with "rheumatic pains and aguish shivering". However, this did not stop him finishing off a short novel, *A Rogue's Life*, which was first serialized in *Household Words* in March of that year; however, it was not finally published in book form until 1879. Furthermore, whilst in Paris, he had bought several second-hand volumes of French forensic and legal proceedings, which provided him with abundant material for many of his later productions, including certain details for one of his masterpieces, *The Woman in White*. On his return he became

113

a staff member of *Household Words*, and collaborated with Dickens on numerous items for the magazine.

1857 saw the publication of his next novel, *The Dead Secret*, his first piece of longer fiction written for serialization. It appeared between January and June in *Household Words*, and was immediately afterwards issued as a book. It received very mixed reviews. In addition, Collins by this time had two plays – *The Frozen Deep* and *The Lighthouse* – in performance on the London stage.

He spent September of that year on a walking tour of the Lake District with Dickens, and collaborated with him in producing a semi-fictionalized account of their experiences in *The Lazy Tour of Two Idle Apprentices*, which was subsequently serialized in *Household Words*. When, in 1858, Dickens's marriage split up, Collins gave him a lot of emotional support.

Caroline Graves   It was at this time that Collins himself at last moved out of his mother's home and began to live openly with a woman who had hardly been mentioned in connection with him before; he lived with her, with only one interruption, for the rest of his life. Her name was Caroline Graves, and she was a widow. She had a daughter called Harriet, commonly referred to as Carrie. Caroline was the daughter of a carpenter, and the widow of a solicitor who had died of consumption. When Wilkie first got to know her, she was running a general-goods store in central London. They never married, and not much is known about the nature of their relationship. Towards the end of his life, Wilkie destroyed many of his letters and personal papers. No letters survive between him and Caroline.

Although Collins was now beginning to make a living by his pen, he was still, by the terms of his father's will, dependent on his mother for any extra money he might need. She took resolutely against this "common shopgirl" whom Wilkie had become embroiled with. She is reputed to have exclaimed, "Never mention that woman's name to me!" Collins seems to have lived on the whole a quiet and settled domestic existence with Caroline and her daughter. The young girl grew especially fond of him, and remained close to him for the rest of his life, even after she had married and moved out.

The Major   The decade after Wilkie began to live with Caroline, *Novels* he reached what is generally agreed to be the apogee of his creativity, with the production of four major novels, including his masterpieces, *The Woman in White* and *The Moonstone*.

Also at this time, Dickens commenced his next publishing venture, the weekly magazine *All the Year Round*, which now superseded *Household Words*. *The Woman in White* was serialized in *All the Year Round* from November 1859 to August 1860, and was then immediately published in book form. It received rave reviews, became a best-seller both in Britain and America, and was translated into all the major European languages. Huge queues gathered outside the magazine's offices on publication day, in order that avid readers could snap up the latest instalment of the story instantly. The novel is considered one of the zeniths of the "sensation novel".

In January 1861, Wilkie resigned from the staff of *All the Year Round*, having acquired a sufficient income from his writing. His next novel, *No Name*, was still serialized in that magazine in 1862 and early 1863. It was published in volume form at the end of 1862 and sold extremely well. In fact the initial print run of 4,000 – very large for the time – was almost entirely sold out on publication day. However, reviews, though once again extolling the style, were damning as to the perceived immorality of the subject matter.

During all of this period Collins was suffering more and more from severe pains caused by his rheumatic illness, and was becoming increasingly dependent on laudanum and other drugs to alleviate the symptoms, which at the time were freely available in any chemist's shop without a prescription. Although he still managed to keep up a punishing schedule, there are already signs in his letters that he was beginning to fear the way in which his drug habit was affecting his writing and his ability to meet deadlines.

For the rest of his life he was constantly trying all kinds of remedies for his ailments, including visits to British and Continental spas, special diets and electromagnetic baths. However, since he refused to give up rich food and fine wine, which were known to exacerbate his condition, these therapies could have only a limited effect.

Wilkie's next novel, *Armadale*, was serialized between 1864 and 1866 in *The Cornhill* – though this move away from *All the Year Around* was only temporary. Once again the book was praised for its style, but damned for its immorality. However, it is now considered to be one of the author's major works. As usual, despite (or perhaps because of) this critical vilification, it sold extremely well.

By 1867, Wilkie was already deep in research for his next novel, *The Moonstone*. The author was by now in such pain, and his eyes – which observers described as being like pools of blood – were so affected, either by his illness or his drug habit, that he could not write, but had to employ a series of scribes, many of whom left within a short time, finding his agonized shrieks and groans unbearable.

Martha Rudd   In March 1868, Wilkie's mother died, and indeed *The Moonstone* is dedicated to her memory. Caroline at last thought the path would be clear for Wilkie to marry her, but then another young woman emerged in Wilkie's life. Martha Rudd was the daughter of a shepherd and came from a large family near Yarmouth in Norfolk. Her father was a shepherd, and the family was a large one. Collins first met her in Yarmouth in 1864, when she was nineteen and working as a servant at the hotel Wilkie was staying at on holiday, in another attempt to alleviate his health problems. She seems to have been a high-spirited, independent and literate young woman. He met her several times more in Yarmouth, and although the early development of their relationship is unclear, she was living in London by 1868, and it was apparent that Collins and she were involved in more than a platonic friendship.

Caroline left Collins, and in October 1868, at the age of thirty-eight, she married the twenty-seven-year-old son of a distiller. Martha became pregnant by Wilkie for the first time, and in 1869 gave birth to a daughter, Marian. She subsequently bore him two further children – in 1871 another daughter, Harriet, and in 1874 a son, William.

In 1871, for unknown reasons, Caroline left her young husband and returned to Collins. She now seems to have been accepted, by those of Wilkie's acquaintances familiar with his private life, as his unofficial wife, while Martha was regarded as his mistress. Wilkie had enough money by now from his writing and his mother's legacy to maintain the two households separately. Martha was always referred to as "Mrs Dawson", possibly to conceal the nature of his relationship with her, and this is the surname the three children were given, which passed down to subsequent descendents. Marriage was no more of a prospect with Martha than it was with Caroline. The innermost workings of his relationship with Martha are extremely unclear, but she seems to have been happy with the arrangement, and the three children adored their father. He showered them with love and gifts, played with them unconstrainedly and, whenever he visited them, kept them spellbound with enthralling tales.

The Moonstone was serialized in *All the Year Round* between January and August 1868, and was published in book form in July of that year. It created a sensation: the reviews were extremely favourable and it was an immediate best-seller on both sides of the Atlantic. It contains prototypical features of much modern detective fiction, such as deliberately misleading clues, a detective from the local police force who fails to solve the crime, red herrings and a final reconstruction of the events on the night of the crime. There is no omniscient single narrator, and the story is only gradually pieced together, as in a court of law, from the reminiscences of several different narrators. *The Moonstone*

After this decade or so of creativity, Collins's narrative fiction is generally agreed to have declined in quality rapidly. The main reason for this was his opium addiction, which made it more and more difficult for him to undertake complex plotting and extended writing. However, another part of the explanation might be that in 1870 he had adapted *The Woman in White* for the stage, with enormous success, both critical and financial, and from now on dramatic versions of his novels began to enjoy ever-increasing acclaim. Collins had claimed early on in his career that plays and novels were intimately linked, and some commentators believe that, from around 1870, the author's novels began to be envisioned not so much as dense narratives, but as series of rapidly succeeding scenes which could very easily be adapted for the stage. Several of his later novels appeared almost simultaneously in stage form. These creations received progressively more scathing reviews. *Later Works*

On 9th June 1870, Dickens died. Collins had benefited immensely from the friendship and guidance of the older novelist, becoming the first and foremost of "Dickens's young men". Collins's laudanum use steadily escalated over this period of time, getting to a point where he used it not only to deal with physical pain, but also to induce sleep. He carried round a large hip flask of laudanum, taking daily doses which would have killed anybody not inured to the drug, and was also having nightmares and hallucinations. *Decline*

On 9th April 1873, Wilkie's younger brother Charles died; he had never succeeded in fulfilling his artistic aspirations, and to the end of his life regarded himself as a failure. In September Collins undertook a six-month tour of the USA and Canada,

117

giving readings from his works and, like Dickens before him in 1867, enactments of the speeches of some of his characters on the stage. The tour had netted Dickens £20,000, but – since the exhausting schedule Dickens had set himself in America was considered to have been a major contributory factor to his relatively early death – Collins (who had by now, in addition to all his other health problems, been diagnosed as having a weak heart) deliberately restricted his appearances. Furthermore, although laudatory articles about his work appeared in the American press, and he was a guest at numerous receptions and banquets, his performances were generally considered to be very disappointing in comparison to those of Dickens. A few members of the audience actually grew bored and walked out early.

However, Wilkie still made a profit from the tour of around £2,500 – an enormous sum for the time – and it gave him enough to keep both his households in comfort, and to provide for them amply after his death. During this period he was constantly falling further and further behind with deadlines, and critics were treating his new works with contempt, questioning whether his lurid inventions were out of step with the times – public taste had moved on.

Death By the 1880s he felt he was falling apart through illness and drugs. He moved to his last home, at 82 Wimpole Street, London, in 1887. One day he went out for his usual short walk, and suddenly found himself unable to breathe and hardly able to stagger home. The symptoms were consistent with those of a heart attack. He managed to celebrate his sixty-fifth birthday in 1889, but, on holiday in Ramsgate in June of that year, he suffered a stroke, and was brought back to Wimpole Street, where his mind grew increasingly more confused, and his physical condition deteriorated rapidly. He realized he would never be able to finish his last novel, *Blind Love*, and so delegated his colleague Walter Besant to complete it from the copious notes and plans he had earlier drawn up. He died on 23rd September 1889. All the letters of condolence were sent to Caroline; Martha and her family were either not known about or ignored.

He is now buried at Kensal Green Cemetery, London, along with many other noted luminaries of the time, such as Anthony Trollope, William Thackeray and Isambard Brunel. His estate was divided equally between Caroline and Carrie on the one hand, and Martha and her family on the other. It came to some £10,832 – a very large sum for the time. The clergymen of both Westminster Abbey and St Paul's Cathedral refused to allow a memorial to be installed in their buildings in his honour, which was the usual mark of respect for outstanding figures of the time. This was presumably because of his unconventional lifestyle, and what was seen as the "immorality" of his books, including their anti-religious element. In June 1895, Caroline died, and was buried in Collins's grave.

Wilkie Collins's Works

Collins wrote over a score each of novels and plays, and more than fifty short stories. Most of the plays, especially during the latter part of the author's career, were adaptations of one of his novels, and they are not considered to be on the same level as his narrative work. The following brief survey will therefore deal only with his novels, most of which were serialized in one of the literary journals of the time, prior to publication in volume form. Although the so-called "sensation novel" element only became predominant in Collins's novels from the 1860s onwards, he was, as mentioned above, always interested in portraying in his works various kinds of physical disability and abnormal mental states; he also had a fascination with mesmerism and an interest in the supernatural. His work after the 1860s is generally considered to have declined drastically in quality, therefore detailed analyses will only be given of the novels until that period.

Collins wrote his first novel, *Iolâni, or Tahiti as It Was: A* *Iolâni* *Romance* in 1844, and submitted it to publishers in 1845. All rejected it, presumably apprehensive as to how its setting among unchristian natives would go down with the public. Although the lurid plot was derived from Collins's own imagination, he did a great deal of research regarding the geographical and historical background – as he did for all of his subsequent novels. For a long time, the novel was thought to be completely lost, but it was rediscovered in 1991, and finally published in 1999. The plot involves evil high priests, illegitimate birth, the custom of killing first-born sons, witch doctors and a wild but noble recluse living in the forest, who saves a baby boy left in the open to die. At the conclusion of the novel, the wild woodman, who is by now totally deranged, forces the evil high priest Iolâni – the father of the baby – to go into a leaking canoe with him, because, it transpires, the recluse was once a victim of the priest's wickedness too. They set out to sea just as a tropical storm is brewing up and presumably die as a result. The baby is brought up in peace by his mother.

Antonina   His second novel, *Antonina, or The Fall of Rome: A Romance of the Fifth Century*, was begun in 1846, delayed while Collins wrote his memoir of his recently deceased father, and finally published in February 1850. This was Collins's first published novel, based on materials in Gibbon's *Decline and Fall of the Roman Empire*, and attempting to capitalize on the fashion for such novels established by Bulwer-Lytton in *The Last Days of Pompeii* (1834). It is written in a deliberately florid style reminiscent of both these earlier authors. The novel received excellent reviews, and was reprinted several times during Collins's lifetime. There was an American edition in 1850 and a translation into German in the same year.

Antonina is the daughter of a wealthy and fanatical Christian household in 408 AD; however, the steward of the house is secretly a pagan, who wishes to restore the old gods. Antonina is captured by a chief of the invading Goths, who falls in love with her. She escapes and finds her way back to Rome and her starving family. The heathen steward, who is by now raving mad, attempts to sacrifice Antonina to the old gods, but after a series of turbulent events she is rescued. The steward now reveals that he is in fact the long-lost brother of Antonina's Christian father; he barricades himself in a disused heathen temple, which the Christians burn down with him inside. Antonina, who is extremely ill after her traumatic experiences, is nursed back to health by her father, and, as the novel fades out peacefully here, the impression is given that she subsequently lives a quiet existence, looking after her father as he enters old age.

Mr Wray's Cash Box   *Mr Wray's Cash Box: A Christmas Sketch* was a short novella written on the model of Dickens's Christmas books, published in January 1852. The frontispiece was by the Pre-Raphaelite painter Millais.

Wray is an impecunious former actor, who retires to the countryside after making a plaster cast of Shakespeare's face, from which he intends to earn a future living by mass-producing more copies. However, the authorities are trying to prove that this is illegal. He keeps this cast in his old cash box. In the end, everything turns out for the best, judgement is given in his favour, and his granddaughter marries his assistant.

Collins's next novel, *Basil: A Story of Modern Life,* was published in November 1852, receiving very mixed reviews; Collins's literary friends, especially Dickens, were extremely enthusiastic, but the critics called it "revolting" and "disgusting". Possibly in response to this outcry, Collins made scores of small amendments to later editions, which toned down the original violence of the novel. *Basil*

Basil, the younger son of an ancient noble family, falls in love with Margaret, a linen-draper's daughter. He follows her home and asks her father whether he can marry her; however, because his own father will object, the marriage must be kept secret. Margaret's father agrees, but asks that the union should not be consummated for a year, since Margaret has only just turned seventeen. Accordingly, they marry, but Basil continues to live at his home, and to visit her under the chaperonage of her mother. As he learns more of her infantile character, he begins to wonder if he has made a mistake. Before the year is out, Margaret becomes emotionally involved with Robert, one of her father's clerks; Basil follows them to a hotel, hides behind a partition, and hears him attempt to seduce her. Basil assaults him, leaving him permanently disfigured, and with the sight of only one eye. Basil then confesses his marriage to his father, who throws him out of the house permanently. Robert now reveals that his own father was hanged for forgery, and that Basil's father could have prevented this, but chose not to do so. For this reason, when Robert discovered who Basil was, and that he was secretly married to Margaret, he resolved to destroy Basil's happiness. Margaret, visiting Robert in hospital, contracts typhus and dies, and Basil forgives her as she is on the point of death. He then leaves London for a long stay in Cornwall, and is confronted by the now mentally unhinged Robert on the cliffs. Robert falls to his death and Basil has a total nervous breakdown. He is reconciled with his father, and retires to the countryside to be tended back to health by his younger sister.

Collins's next novel, *Hide and Seek*, published in June 1854, was dedicated to Charles Dickens, who wrote, "I think it far away the cleverest novel I have ever seen written by a new hand." It generally received excellent reviews, but sales *Hide and Seek* were poor. It is the first Collins novel to explore the role of physical disability: the heroine is deaf and dumb. Mary, often called Madonna because of her beauty, is the adopted deaf-and-dumb daughter of an artist and his invalid wife. Nobody knows who her real parents were, as she was brought up in a travelling circus. The young Zach Thorpe is a frequent visitor at the house of Madonna's parents, and she falls in love with him. However, he lives a dissipated and drunken life, and does not respond to her love. After many convolutions of plot, it transpires that Zach's father is also Madonna's father; he had seduced Madonna's mother and abandoned her. Zach goes travelling to America, and, finally having matured, returns home to settle down peacefully.

The Dead Secret   *The Dead Secret* was his first novel specifically written for serialization before publication in book form. It appeared between January and June 1857 in *Household Words*, and was published in volume form in June of that year. The story has another disabled hero, a blind man. The extraordinarily complicated plot commences with deathbed confessions, which were written down and then promptly hidden; they are rediscovered many years later, when it transpires that the wife of the blind hero, Rosamond, has finally rightfully inherited a vast fortune.

The Woman in White   Serialized from November 1859 to August 1860 in Dickens's successor publication to *Household Words*, *All the Year Round*, *The Woman in White* was published in book form in August 1860. Often regarded as one of the first sensation novels, *The Woman in White* engendered many imitations and adaptations. Reviews were extraordinarily favourable, and enthusiastic readers included Prince Albert, Gladstone and Thackeray. What today would be called "spin-off marketing" capitalized on the novel's popularity by naming items of clothing and scents after the novel. There were even "Woman in White Waltzes" specially composed to be danced at balls. The story was published almost simultaneously in America, and was swiftly translated into all the major European languages. The book employs a theme that was to become more and more common in Collins's works – that of switched identity.

Walking home from Hampstead in north London before leaving to take up a post in Cumberland, a young art teacher, Walter Hartright, meets a mysterious and deeply distressed young woman dressed in white, whose name is Anne

Catherick; she has apparently escaped from an asylum for the mentally ill. It has been suggested that the original source for the character of Anne was Caroline Graves. On arriving in Cumberland, Walter takes up his post at the mansion of the wealthy Mr Fairlie as art teacher to Laura, his niece, and her half-sister Marian. He notices that Laura is extraordinarily similar to Anne, who, it transpires, had lived in Cumberland as a child, and had been very fond of Laura's now dead mother, who used to dress her in white.

Hartright and Laura fall in love, but she has already been promised to the sinister Sir Percival Glyde, whom she subsequently marries. However, Hartright becomes convinced that Sir Percival was responsible for confining Anne in the lunatic asylum for no reason. Glyde and his wife return to his family estate in Hampshire, and he is accompanied by his even more villainous friend, the foreign Count Fosco. Glyde, it now emerges, is in severe financial difficulties, and he tries to bully Laura into making over all of her substantial marriage settlement to him.

While investigating all of this, Marian is caught in the rain and becomes seriously ill. Laura is tricked into travelling to London, and the identities of Anne and Laura are then switched. Anne dies of a heart condition and Laura is drugged and placed in the asylum under Anne's name. When Marian recovers, she visits the asylum, believing she will meet Anne and learn something about the case, only to discover Laura, whom she aids to escape.

Hartright re-emerges onto the scene, and all three live in secrecy, determined to expose the conspiracy. While investigating, Hartright discovers that Glyde is in fact illegitimate, and is therefore not the rightful heir to the estate, and has forged the marriage register in the nearby church to conceal this fact. Glyde tries to destroy the relevant register to hide his wrongdoing, but accidentally sets the church on fire and dies in the flames. Hartright further discovers that Anne was the illegitimate child of Laura's father, so they are half-sisters. Laura's true identity is proved, she marries Hartright, and their son becomes rightful heir of the family estate.

No Name, Collins's next novel, was serialized in *All the Year Round* from March 1862 to January 1863, and published in book form in December 1862. Although arguably not on the artistic level of *The Woman in White* or *The Moonstone*, *No*

No Name

123

Name is still considered to be one of Collins's four major novels. Following the success of *The Woman in White*, the first print run of *No Name* was 4,000 – very large for the time – which almost sold out on the first day it appeared. The novel's theme is illegitimacy: two middle-class sisters, products of what has seemed a happy and secure marriage, discover to their horror, when both of their parents suddenly die unexpectedly, that they had never in fact married, and that therefore they can inherit nothing, not even the family name. After very many twists and turns, the sisters discover who their true friends are, who have not abandoned them despite their reduced status, and both make financially secure marriages.

Armadale   The next of the four great novels published from 1859 to 1868, *Armadale* is Collins's longest and possibly most complex novel. It was serialized in *The Cornhill Magazine* from November 1864 to June 1866 and appeared in book form in May 1866. Once again, Collins's work was praised for the quality of the writing, but lambasted for its subject matter; one review called the heroine "a woman fouler than the refuse of the streets", and another described her as "one of the most hardened female villains whose devices and desires have ever blackened fiction".

A measure of the complexity of the plot is that there are four characters called Allan Armadale, two of them of the older generation, two of the younger. The older Allans are cousins, and one murders the other. The murderer discovers that the cousin he has murdered has fathered a child. He, the murderer, then flees to Barbados, and marries a lady of mixed Afro-Caribbean and European blood, by whom he has a child. Both children also bear the name Allan. This means, interestingly, that one younger Armadale is very pale and fair, because both his parents were British, whereas the other, the product of the liaison of the murderer with a woman of mixed blood, is very dark. The dark Allan, who lives in Britain under the pseudonym Ozias Midwinter, turns out to be highly principled, kind and trustworthy – almost the only person in the book to be so – whereas the white son of the murdered man is naive, gullible and at first rather dissolute.

On his deathbed, the murderer writes a confession to be given to his son, "dark" Armadale, when he comes of age. In England, Midwinter loses his job because of illness, and is shown great kindness by his white cousin – although of course they do not realize their kinship at this stage. They strike up a close friendship, and it is at this stage that Midwinter is given his father's letter and realizes that his friend is in fact his cousin, and that his father murdered white Armadale's father. Midwinter burns the letter, vowing to keep the secret for ever. Midwinter, while remaining close to Armadale to protect him from the various intrigues against him by people who are trying to deprive him of his inheritance, does not reveal his identity. Following an attempt to murder white Allan by filling his room with gas – which merely succeeds in almost killing dark Allan – white Allan marries and lives happily ever after. The novel ends with Midwinter embarking on a long journey abroad, from which he intends to return to try to make a career as an author. He never reveals the blood relationship between himself and his friend, although it appears they will be close acquaintances for ever.

The Moonstone was serialized in *All the Year Round* from *The Moonstone* January to August 1868 and was published in book form in three volumes in July 1868. Almost simultaneously with its appearance in *All the Year Round* in London, the tale was serialized in *Harper's Magazine* in America. It was dedicated to the memory of the author's mother Harriet, who died on 19th March 1868. Reviews were mixed, but interest in the novel was extraordinary.

Collins undertook an enormous amount of research preparatory to writing the novel, principally at the library of his London club, the Athenaeum. He took copious notes from the 1855 edition of *Encyclopaedia Britannica*, *The Natural History of Gems* by C.W. King, *The History of India from the Earliest Ages* by J. Talboys Wheeler and many other volumes. He also consulted noted orientalists and explorers of the Indian subcontinent for historical and cultural background material. Collins's original title was *The Serpent's Eye*.

During the writing of the story, Collins was suffering from an especially severe and painful attack of his "rheumatic gout", and the novel was falling dangerously behind schedule due to the author's attendance at the bedside of his dying mother. He took vast amounts of laudanum to keep himself going and finished the novel utterly burnt-out physically and mentally.

Collins claimed later that some sections of the novel, including the epilogue, were written when he was in such a laudanum-induced haze that he did not recognize them as his own – although he was extremely pleased with the result.

The story starts with the account of the original theft of the Moonstone from Seringapatam by John Herncastle. The action then jumps forwards in time to Franklin Blake taking the Moonstone to Rachel Verinder: she has inherited it from Herncastle, and we are led to doubt the generosity of his motives in doing so, due to the supposed curse surrounding the jewel. Rachel wears the jewel on her birthday, but fails to put it in a secure place when she goes to bed. In the morning, it is gone; the police are called and suspicion falls on three Indian travellers who have recently visited the house. Also present on the occasion of the jewel's theft is Godfrey Ablewhite, a public philanthropist, who competes for Rachel's romantic affections with Franklin Blake. The local police officer in charge of the inquiry, Superintendent Seegrave, proving to be incompetent, Franklin Blake, who is very active in helping the investigation, recruits another officer to take charge of things – the renowned Sergeant Cuff from London. Sergeant Cuff inspects all aspects of the case and identifies as the key to the mystery a blotch on a recently painted door caused by contact with a nightdress. Suspicion falls on one of the servants, Rosanna Spearman, whose behaviour has been unusual recently. However, before this line of the investigation reaches an end, Rosanna kills herself by jumping into a pit of quicksand. Cuff tries to continue his investigation, but is stopped by Lady Verinder, Rachel's mother, when his insights lead him to the idea that Rachel herself is the culprit, aided by her loyal servant, Rosanna. Since the theft of her diamond, Rachel has been behaving strangely, not cooperating with the investigation and warding off her suitors, Ablewhite and Blake. She leaves the country house and goes to live in London, and Blake goes abroad in order to try to forget about Rachel. While in London, Rachel accepts Ablewhite's marriage proposal, but later reneges.

Some years later, Blake returns to England, determined at last to find out the truth about the Moonstone. He returns to Lady Verinder's house in Yorkshire, the site of the theft. There he manages, by following a series of clues, to find the nightdress which made the blotch on the door. He discovers, to his horror and bafflement, that it is actually his own. While staying in Yorkshire, Blake becomes acquainted with Ezra Jennings, a local doctor's assistant with an unusual and striking appearance. He discusses the case in detail with Ezra, who is able to come up with a solution, through clues left by the doctor senior to him, who was there on the night in question. Ezra proposes a radical interpretation – that the doctor had secretly administered opium to Blake on the night in question, and that Blake had taken the jewel while in an opium-induced trance, which left no memory of the deed. In order to test this theory, they attempt to duplicate the conditions of the night of the deed. The experiment is largely successful, proving to their satisfaction Ezra's conjecture. Blake and Rachel Verinder are reconciled – her reasons for rejecting him were to do with the events of the night of the theft and she is now convinced of his innocence on the matter.

Mr Bruff, Blake's lawyer, is convinced that the jewel is in London, being held securely by a banker there. However, it is removed from the bank, and traced by Mr Bruff and his associates to a room above a public house. At the same time, it appears that the three Indians have now reappeared on the scene. Sergeant Cuff has become involved in the investigation again, and is now convinced that his original view of Rachel's guilt was wrong – he now suspects another person present on the night. The room above the public house is broken into, and they find the dead body of Godfrey Ablewhite. The Moonstone is gone, but there is evidence of its presence and removal – it is now certain that the three Indians took it. Attempts to trace their movements and recover the Moonstone fail. In the final pages, it appears in India, where it rightfully belongs.

After *The Moonstone*, Collins's output is commonly agreed to have gone into catastrophic decline, as mentioned above. His novels now became vehicles for his views on life and society, and they became more and more boringly didactic; as the poet Algernon Swinburne put it: "What brought good Wilkie's genius nigh perdition? / Some demon whispered "Wilkie! have a mission."

The first such novel was *Man and Wife*, serialized from *Man and Wife* January 1870, and published in book form in June 1870. The story attacks antiquated marriage laws, and also pours scorn on the prevailing cult of clean living and healthy athleticism. One review mocked this high-minded didacticism by saying that if one moral was generally too much, two were surely unjustifiable. The plot concerns abandoned wives, secret marriages, women whose marital status is legally dubious due to loopholes in the law, and a woman struck dumb by the combined stress of a traumatic marriage, attempted murder and confinement in an asylum.

Poor Miss Finch   Then came *Poor Miss Finch*, serialized from October 1871 to March 1872, the book form appearing in February. In the novel, a wealthy young blind woman – the Miss Finch of the title – falls in love with a neighbour, Oscar, who has an identical twin brother, Nugent. Following a vicious attack, Oscar becomes severely epileptic. He undergoes a revolutionary treatment which has the effect of permanently staining his skin dark blue. There is a plot to marry Miss Finch to the identical brother Nugent, but she detects the deception through her other senses. She marries Oscar, because, of course, his weird bright blue appearance makes no difference to her, as she cannot see it. Nugent joins an Arctic expedition and freezes to death, clutching a lock of Miss Finch's hair.

The New Magdalen   Collins then had *The New Magdalen* serialized in *Temple Bar* magazine from October 1872 to May 1873; it appeared in book form in May 1873. In the novel, a tragic but noble-hearted prostitute called Mercy, inspired by the preachings of a young clergyman, strives to give up her way of life by working as a nurse in the Franco-Prussian war of 1870. There she establishes a friendship with the virtuous and well-connected Grace, who has no near family, but only distant relatives who have never seen her. When Grace is apparently killed by a shell blast, Mercy assumes her identity and becomes, on her return to Britain, the accepted relation and companion of a wealthy titled lady. Grace, however, has recovered against all the odds and returns, only to be rejected as an impostor. Mercy, once more under the influence of the same clergyman whose original preaching converted her, now confesses her wrongdoing. The clergyman becomes seriously ill, Mercy nurses him back to health and they marry and sail to a new life in America.

The Law and the Lady   The novel *The Law and the Lady* was serialized in *The Graphic* from September 1874 to March 1875, then published in book form in February 1875. The novel has a very complex plot involving an amateur female detective, family secrets, murders and a sinister manic depressive with no legs.

The Two Destinies   His next novel, *The Two Destinies*, appeared in *Harper's Bazaar* from December 1875 to September 1876, and was published in volume form in August 1876. This novel concerns

128   two childhood sweethearts, whose destinies are inextricably

linked, according to people with the gift of clairvoyance. After they are forcibly separated by their families, the female sweetheart, whose appearance has been utterly transformed by illness, throws herself into a river, but is saved by the male sweetheart, who just happens to be passing on his return, after many years in India, to inherit an estate. Although they fail to recognize each other, they become almost telepathically at one, and both of them have supernatural visions of each other imploring a meeting. After several more plot twists and supernatural visions, they finally recognize each other, are married and leave England to start life afresh in Italy.

The first novel of *The Fallen Leaves* series appeared in *The World* from January to July 1879, and then in book form in July 1879. The "fallen leaves" are, he explained, "the people who have drawn blanks in the lottery of life... the friendless and the lonely, the wounded and the lost." Four women – all "fallen leaves" – have guilty secrets, and are all involved in some way or another with the improbably named Amelius Greatheart. The novel, dedicated to Caroline Graves, received such contemptuous reviews that Collins never produced a second series. *The Fallen Leaves*

The fall in popularity of Collins's novels is exemplified by the fact that, from this point on, all his novels were serialized before publication in regional newspapers, rather than the London literary magazines. *Jezebel's Daughter* was serialized in the *Bolton Weekly Journal* from September 1879 to January 1880, the book form appearing in March 1880. The melodramatic plot involves another rehash of the by now familiar themes: poisonings, embezzlement, detective work and mentally disturbed and disabled people. *Jezebel's Daughter*

Initially serialized in several regional newspapers, notably *The Sheffield and Rotherham Independent Supplement* from October 1880 to March 1881, *The Black Robe* appeared in book form in April 1881. It is an anti-Jesuit and anti-Catholic piece, concerning a Catholic clergyman who schemes unsuccessfully to recover, by various dishonest means, a monastery which was lost to the Catholic Church and is now owned by a wealthy private family. *The Black Robe*

Again serialized only in the regional newspapers, principally the *Manchester Weekly Times Supplement* from July 1882 to January 1883, Collins's next offering, *Heart and Science*, appeared in book form in April 1883. It is an anti-vivisection *Heart and Science* novel with a hero called Ovid, whose mother remarries under the name of Mrs Galilee; other main characters are named Carmina and Miss Minerva. It tells the story of a villainous vivisectionist, who realizes his life's work is a failure, releases his captive animals, destroys his laboratory by fire, and perishes in the flames. Another plot strand is about Mrs Galilee having a nervous breakdown, but eventually recovering, and a further one is about Ovid and Carmina marrying.

I Say No   Collins's following novel, *I Say No*, was serialized in regional newspapers, principally the *Glasgow Weekly Herald* from December 1883 to July 1884, and published in volume form in October 1884. It is a mystery story with themes of forgery, an apparent murder and another female amateur detective.

The Evil Genius   Next, instalments of *The Evil Genius* appeared in numerous regional newspapers between December 1885 and May 1886, principally in the *Leigh Journal and Times* and the *Bolton Weekly Journal*, with the volume edition published four months after the end of serialization. The evil genius of the title is an interfering mother-in-law, and the plot deals with adultery and divorce.

The Guilty River   Collins then published a short novel entitled *The Guilty River* in November 1886 as a Christmas story. A deaf man, known only as the Lodger, tries to poison the hero, Gerard, because The Lodger is in love with Cristel, Gerard's beloved. Cristel subsequently disappears, and so does the Lodger; in the end, the dying Lodger confesses that Cristel has been abducted by her father and Gerard's wealthy relations and friends, who do not approve of his marrying a girl who is *The Legacy of Cain*   below him in station.

The last novel Collins ever completed was *The Legacy of Cain*. Serialized in various regional newspapers, principally the *Leigh Journal and Times*, from February to June 1888, it appeared in book form in November 1888 and was dedicated to Carrie Graves (by now Mrs Bartley), the author's stepdaughter. The plot concerns what Collins believed to be the erroneous notion of hereditary wickedness; the Reverend Abel Gracedieu, has two daughters: one his own, and one adopted. The adoptive daughter has been kept in ignorance of her antecedents, because it is believed her mother was executed for murdering her husband. There are ghostly visions and, among other incidents, the vicar becomes mentally deranged and attempts to kill a prison governor with a razor, while the sister, who we have been led to believe has bad blood, tries to poison her unfaithful lover. She serves a short term in prison, and emigrates to America, where she becomes the leader of a women's religious cult. It transpires near the end of the novel that, in fact, the evil sister is not the adoptive daughter of the murderess, but her virtuous sister is; this upright and honourable young woman was adopted by the Reverend Gracedieu as part of his Christian duty when her mother was executed.

Another novel, unfinished by Collins, entitled *Blind Love*, *Blind Love* was published posthumously in 1890, completed by Wilkie's friend Walter Besant on the basis of the author's copious plans and notes. "Blind Love" refers not to another character with a handicap, but to a virtuous heroine who is blinded by her love for an aristocratic villain. He is finally murdered by Fenian terrorists.

In addition to his novels, Wilkie Collins achieved great *Major Plays* success with his plays, most of which, as we have seen above, were adaptations of his prose writings. Collins's most important dramatic works are arguably the following: *A Court Duel* (1850), *The Lighthouse* (1855), *The Frozen Deep* (1857), *The Red Vial* (1858), *The Woman in White* (1860), *A Message from the Sea* (in collaboration with Dickens, 1861), *No Name* (1866, rewritten in 1870), *Armadale* (1866), *No Thoroughfare* (in collaboration with Dickens, 1867), *Black and White* (1869), *Man and Wife* (1870), *The New Magdalen* (1873), *Miss Gwilt* (1875), *The Moonstone* (1877), *Rank and Riches* (1883).

Select Bibliography

Biographies:
Clarke, W.M., *The Secret Life of Wilkie Collins* (London: Allison & Busby, 1988)
Davis, Nuel Pharr, *The Life of Wilkie Collins* (Urbana, IL: University of Illinois Press, 1956)
Peters, Catherine, *The King of Inventors: A Life of Wilkie Collins* (London: Secker & Warburg, 1991)
Robinson, Kenneth, *Wilkie Collins: A Biography* (London: Bodley Head, 1951)

Additional Background Material:

Baker, William and Gasson, Andrew, eds., *The Public Face of Wilkie Collins: The Collected Letters,* 4 vols. (London: Pickering & Chatto, 2005).

Gasson, Andrew, ed., *Wilkie Collins: An Illustrated Guide* (Oxford: Oxford University Press, 1998)

Page, Norman, ed., *Wilkie Collins The Critical Heritage* (London & Boston: Routledge and Kegan Paul, 1974)

Pykett, Lyn, *Wilkie Collins* (Oxford: Oxford University Press, 2005)

Taylor, Jenny Bourne, ed., *The Cambridge Companion to Wilkie Collins* (Cambridge: Cambridge University Press, 2006)

On the Web:
www.wilkiecollins.com

ALMA CLASSICS

ALMA CLASSICS aims to publish mainstream and lesser-known European classics in an innovative and striking way, while employing the highest editorial and production standards. By way of a unique approach the range offers much more, both visually and textually, than readers have come to expect from contemporary classics publishing.

LATEST TITLES PUBLISHED BY ALMA CLASSICS

To order any of our titles and for up-to-date information about our current and forthcoming publications, please visit our website on:

www.almaclassics.com